**Meet Winchester Prep**

I looked down the hall and n people who had never been was talking animatedly to a girl I didn't recog when Mr Ezhno strode out of the classroom.

"Miss Duke." He closed the door behind him. "I know we've had this conversation many times before, but you still don't come in on time and honestly I don't know what more I can do..."

I stopped listening. He was right; we had had this conversation so many times. He would prattle on about how it was not only disrespectful to him but also to my classmates, and so on, and then try to relate to me by telling me a story from his youth.

I shifted my focus back to the pair I'd been watching before Mr Ezhno had come out. They were still there in front of the office, Liam talking enthusiastically to the girl I didn't recognise. She said something that was apparently just *hilarious*, and he laughed appreciatively.

My chest tightened, the way it always did when I saw Liam. It had been such a long time since he'd ended things, and yet it still broke my heart a little to see him talking to another girl. I strained to hear them, knowing that a hundred yards was definitely out of my earshot. And then I caught the tail end of something Mr Ezhno was saying.

"...expulsion."

*Wait. What?*

# here lies Bridget

PAIGE HARBISON

Published in Great Britain 2011
MIRA Books, Eton House, 18-24 Paradise Road,
Richmond, Surrey, TW9 1SR



ISBN 978 0 7783 0499 9

47-0711

MIRA's policy is to use papers that are natural, renewable and recyclable products and made from wood grown in sustainable forests. The logging and manufacturing processes conform to the legal environmental regulations of the country of origin.

Printed and bound by
CPI Group (UK) Ltd, Croydon, CR0 4YY

For Mommy and Grandmommy,
who helped me learn the easy way.

Also to anyone who has ever had to pay for their
mistakes, or wished someone else would

# PROLOGUE

I pressed down on the accelerator. It felt good to have power back in my life. Even if it was just power over my car, or power over my fate: dying or living.

The road was a winding one, with trees on either side, and very little traffic. I watched the speedometer reading rise from thirty mph to forty.

All I could think about was how sorry everyone would be when they found out. I pictured the local news coverage, the headlines, the sheet of paper they'd send around the school, offering grief counseling to my classmates.

Forty-five.

Maybe it wasn't that I wanted to die; maybe I just wanted to scare them. I wanted them all to realize what could have happened and to feel awful for how they'd acted. I wanted them to try to apologize and beg for a chance to make up for everything they'd done.

Fifty.

Fifty-five.

I pictured the faces of my friends as they heard the news. Grasping each other's arms, waiting to be told everything would be okay. Then hearing that it wouldn't be, or that the doctors weren't sure. Maybe visiting my hospital room, where I would lie motionless, the sound of my heart monitor beeping not nearly often enough.

I wondered who would visit me, who would refuse to leave until I woke up. Perhaps even get into a nasty snarl with one of the doctors who told them to leave because visiting hours were over.

I pictured Meredith having to explain to my father what had happened while he was out of town. She'd admit how she'd treated me, and my father would tell her not to speak to him. Maybe he'd even kick her out of the house. Maybe he'd feel guilty for never being around.

And what if I did die? Who would go to my funeral? Who would read the eulogies? What smiling picture of me would they place in the flower wreath next to my casket? Who would break down while deciding which outfit to wear to the service?

I pictured Liam giving a eulogy for me, vowing never to love again.

My engine roared, my tires eating up the pavement.

I had been paying more attention to my thoughts than to the road, and when I shook my focus back to my driving, I found myself coming too fast into a curve. My foot jerked from the accelerator to the brake in an instinct to survive. Suddenly I wished I could take back the thoughts I'd just had. They were stupid. I was being reckless. I didn't want to die. I wanted to drive back to school and pretend I'd never left at all.

The side of the road veered down an embankment, where the only things that could stop me were the trees.

In seconds, the car tires bounced over the edge of the road into the grass and rocks. My foot, still pressed hard on the brake, shook like a muscle rarely used. I didn't know if I was screaming. All I knew was that my side of the car was heading toward a huge tree.

*Oh, my God, I'm going to die.* Icy fingers clutched my heart.

What happened after that I'd never be able to explain.

I don't know if it was a dream, I don't know if it was real, I don't know if it was my Oz. But it wasn't what I would have expected.

There were no three ghosts, no big silver screen with the movie of my life playing, no well-intentioned angel looking to earn his wings. Just a jury of people I'd wronged, deciding whether or not I got to live.

Everything was done. I couldn't take it back, couldn't change it. It was way too late to say the two words that could have saved me if I'd just meant them sooner.

I'm sorry.

I'm sorry.

I'm sorry…

But we'll get to that. First I have to tell you why I got in the car to begin with.

# CHAPTER ONE

Nothing interesting ever happens or begins on a Thursday.

Friday and Saturday are the weekend. Sunday is the end of the weekend, the last day of rest. Monday is the beginning of another week. Tuesday's a cool name. Wednesday is "hump day," an expression I loathe.

But Thursday is nothing. Everything that's going to happen during the week is over, and the weekend is coming but it's not there yet. Even that old rhyme about the day you were born just says *Thursday's child has far to go.*

What does that even *mean?*

When I woke up that day, I had no idea the day that lay before me was the beginning of the end. There was no strange weather event, the neighborhood dogs weren't howling, no meteors struck Earth.

Maybe if I could have read the shreds of cereal at the bottom of my bowl like tea leaves, I would have gone back to bed. Or just transferred to the local public school right then. Instead, I ate the stupid cereal, drank the crappy coffee my stepmother made (fair trade=bitter and thin in my book) and idly checked to make sure my phone was charged.

Same as every day.

Then, just like every day, I left the bowl by the sink and glanced at the clock on the stove. It read 7:05 a.m. I still had ten minutes before I had to leave for school. Just enough time to double-check my makeup and outfit. I'd started toward the stairs to my room when I heard my stepmother's high heels clopping into the kitchen.

"Hey, Bridget?"

I sighed audibly.

"What?" I had like a million things I'd rather do with my ten minutes than stand here waiting for her to stumble her way through yet another awkward conversation.

"Well..." She came into view at the bottom of the stairs. "I was just thinking that maybe...if you're not doing anything tonight, then maybe we could go see that new movie. The one you couldn't see with your friends because of your father's banquet the other night? *Carriage?*"

She shrugged her thin shoulders under the silk Michael Kors top I would have killed for. Sometimes I looked at her and thought she might be prettier than I was.

I hated that.

"I just figured with your father being out of town until next weekend, maybe we could have sort of a girls' night out." She gave me a tentative smile and waited for a response, and then after not getting one in reasonable time, kept talking. "I looked it up and it sounds pretty good, actually..."

"I have no idea what you're talking about, but I'm busy tonight."

I started up the stairs. I knew exactly which movie she was talking about, and I had been dying to see it. But going to the movies with your stepmother—how pathetic is that? She might as well have asked me to go to a midnight opening of *Blue's Clues 3-D* in full furry costume regalia.

"Oh, but you were so disappointed when you couldn't go the other night..."

I stopped when she said that and bent toward her,

talking to her as if she were the child and *I* was the evil stepmother. "That's because I didn't want to go to Dad's stupid dinner thing, that's all."

"Oh." She looked down at a piece of paper in her hand, which looked like it had the movie summary on it. I felt a small stab of guilt when I saw it.

She folded it in half and followed me as I walked up the stairs. I could feel her eyes on my back. "Well, maybe there's another movie you'd like to see, or we could do something else—"

I stopped and turned again, feeling disproportionately averse to the idea. "Okay, Meredith? I don't know how to make this obvious to you if you really don't get it yet. I don't want to do anything with you tonight. Mmkay?"

Her eyes widened and she looked like she was about to have another one of her crying fits. For God's sake, what was *wrong* with her? She cried all the time lately. She was, like, forty. Was that too young to go into menopause?

Whatever. I wasn't going to take responsibility for upsetting her. I'd walked away from arguments like this feeling guilty before. Walked away feeling like I must have really pushed the limit to make her cry. But then, later in the week, I'd see her sobbing over *Sesame Street* and realize it was not about me.

Though I did wonder why on earth she was alone in the living room watching *Sesame Street.*

I DROVE TO MY BORING, stuffy, private high school, Winchester Preparatory, in my 2007 Toyota Corolla (my father gave me his old car instead of buying me a new one in one of his few-and-far-between fits of parenting) and parked in my usual spot. I was late, also as usual, though this time it was because of the conversation with Meredith. So it wasn't actually my fault. It never is.

Still, I guess I wasn't exactly running down the hall. And I did stop at the vending machines to get a Vitaminwater. After a moment or two of deliberation between flavors, I headed to class. To Tech Ed, where my teacher was as useless as the subject.

His name was Mr. Ezhno, and he was just simply not cut out for teaching. He was weak and spineless, and on top of that, entirely boring. He blathered on, teaching us things everyone in our day and age already knows. How to turn on a computer. How to open a blank document.

When we weren't doing that, we were doing things

like building light switches. Which was stupid, in my opinion. Why should we have to figure it out when it's already *been* figured out? I seriously doubted that I'd ever be in a situation where someone was saying, "Quick, it's an emergency, put down those matches and build a light switch!"

It would have been almost impossible to pay attention to him even if anyone had tried.

Which, naturally, we didn't.

On days when we were behind the computers, we were either working on essays with useless topics or ignoring him to play games or browse the internet, while the more studious students did work for other (real) classes. Either way, none of us were doing what we were supposed to.

About halfway through the semester, he noticed that no one was paying attention to him, so he started making us turn off the computer screens when we weren't supposed to be doing something with them. All this did, however, was bore us into terrorizing him. We would raise our hands and ask deliberately stupid questions, and he would have to answer them, just in case one of them was for real.

Except, there was one day when Matt Churchill had asked, with a completely straight face, if there was really such thing as a "chick magnet." Mr. Ezhno had refused to answer, calling it a "ridiculous question."

But I'd seen the doubt flicker through his eyes as he wondered if Matt was serious.

As if the curriculum wasn't irritating enough, the class was first thing in the morning, making it positively impossible for me to ever get there on time. And once I did get there, I admittedly gave him kind of a hard time.

Every once in a while, a twinge of pity for the man stopped me in my tracks. Him, with his button-down shirts and pleated khakis, his office supplies, weekly boxes of new chalk and the stickers he put on papers with good grades (which, incidentally, I knew existed only from spotting them on other people's papers). He was the classic nerdy teacher. Seriously, if the makers of that movie *Office Space* had seen this guy, they would have given Milton and his stapler the boot and asked Mr. Ezhno to step in.

Often, however, I didn't stop. It usually started with me saying something double-sided that Mr. Ezhno couldn't respond to appropriately. He'd then send me to the main office, I'd get in-school suspension, my behavior wouldn't improve and then he'd have *several* parent-teacher meetings with Meredith.

I hated that.

She was *not* my parent, and my father never got involved in this stuff. Thank *God*.

Still, they would meet, get along and, as I imagined it, plot ways to make my life more frustrating. Luckily, the meetings had stopped somewhere along the way. At this point it was like he'd given up. Which worked for me. Honestly, I'd been about to ease up on him—I could tell I was pushing him too far, and the last thing I needed was to get in trouble. But that didn't seem to be an issue anymore.

So it was 7:40 on *that* Thursday morning when I waltzed into the classroom and crossed right in front of Mr. Ezhno, my shoulder grazing his grade book. I headed toward my seat next to Jillian Orman. I heard the boys in the back row talking about me, saying something sexist but still flattering.

But this time, as opposed to every other time, Mr. Ezhno stopped talking to the class.

His eyes fastened on me.

"Go on." I raised my eyebrows at him, like I was giving him permission, and then twisted open my Vitaminwater.

"Miss Duke, can you please go wait out in the hall for me?" He sounded tired.

"Already?" Snickers from the class, who appreciated my anticipation of getting in trouble—just not yet. "But Mr. Ezhno, I bought the flavor that's supposed to help me focus. I bought it just for your class, Mr. Ezhno." I raised my drink, tapping lightly on the label where it said *Focus*.

Most of the people in the class sniggered quietly, waiting for him to come up with something to say.

Instead he just pointed toward the door.

When I looked at him like I didn't know what he was talking about, he repeated, "Please go wait for me in the hall."

I sighed theatrically and walked out, making a face at his back as soon as I was past him. A ripple of muffled laughs ran through the class.

As I waited for him in the hall, I watched people passing by. Some were on the way to the bathroom, some were late for class and a few probably had first period as an office assistant. I didn't know all of their names, but they always seemed to know me. One girl quickened her pace as she drew closer to me, keeping her eyes directed at her feet. She glanced up, and the second our eyes locked, she looked away.

A moment later another girl walked by wearing a T-shirt from last year's student government election, the faded letters reading *Duke for SGA President!* The election from which I, sensing more support for my fellow candidates, had withdrawn my name, claiming that it was because I had too many other things to worry about.

The girl (Suzanne?) waved, indicated her T-shirt, pointed at me and smiled. I smiled superficially back and watched her go. My own face smiled at me from the back of the shirt.

Kinda weird to wear that sort of thing post-election.

Others who walked by either waved enthusiastically or did the same as the first girl and tried hard not to look at me. That was how it usually was in my life: People were either overly friendly (possibly obsessive) or painfully shy.

Here's why. My father was once a promising young superstar in the NFL until one fateful game where he blew out his knee. Being a good-looking favorite, he then rose to fame as a sportscaster. Every man knew him, every boy wanted to be him, every woman and girl stopped crossing the living room when he was on TV just to watch him finish his segment. Including me. Sometimes I saw him more often on my TV than sitting in front of it.

Anyway, his fame made me cool by association. I didn't need to be head cheerleader (which is good because I never could be), or SGA president (which is what I told myself when I dropped out of the race).

I was a local princess.

I had just looked down the hall to notice one of the few people who had never been fazed by my reputation talking animatedly to a girl I didn't recognize at all when Mr. Ezhno strode out of the classroom.

"Miss Duke." He closed the door behind him. "I know we've had this conversation many times before, but you still don't come in on time and honestly I don't know what more I can do..."

I stopped listening. He was right; we had had this conversation *so* many times. He would prattle on about how it was not only disrespectful to him but also to my classmates, and so on, and then try to relate to me by telling me a story from his youth.

I shifted my focus back to the pair I'd been watching before Mr. Ezhno had come out. They were still there in front of the office, Liam talking enthusiastically to the girl I didn't recognize. She said something that was apparently just *hilarious,* and he laughed appreciatively.

My chest tightened, the way it always did when I saw Liam. It had been such a long time since he'd ended things, and yet it still broke my heart a little to see him talking to another girl. I strained to hear them, knowing that a hundred yards was definitely out of my earshot. And then I caught the tail end of something Mr. Ezhno was saying.

"…expulsion."

Wait, *what?*

I *must* have misheard. "Excuse me?"

He closed his eyes for a few seconds before responding.

"I said that your repeated insubordination and frequent tardiness haven't stopped, despite all of our discussions on the matter. I'm going to have to send you to the office, and frankly, after being late so many times—" he raised his hands for a second, in a movement I knew to mean *What else can I do?* "—the usual punishment is expulsion."

My dad would kill me. *Kill* me. This was the kind of thing that had led to him giving me an old car instead of a new one and suspending my credit cards. Every now and then he'd say something embarrassing on the air about how he thought the Giants were a shoo-in, back to you Rob, and he had to get home to his insubordinate daughter.

"Well, frankly, *Mr. Ezhno…*" I said his name like it

was absurd, like he'd asked us to call him "Mr. Snuggle-kins" or something "...I think that the time we waste having our '*discussions on the matter*—'" I put his words in sarcastic finger quotes "—is a lot more distracting to the class than when I'm late by, like, thirty seconds. I mean, what, do you think that they're studying in there?" I pointed a finger toward the classroom.

When he kept looking at me, I pursed my lips and nodded, like I was trying to convince him to buy something that looked great on him.

As if.

"Just...take this and go to the office." He handed me a folded piece of paper. I could see the imprint of some of the words on the reverse side.

I glanced at him and gave him a look that said something like *your loss* and walked toward the office.

I felt a small drop in my stomach when I saw that Liam and the girl were gone. Fine, there would be no strutting dismissively past them, then.

As I walked down the hall, I read the note.

> Miss Duke has been a constant distraction to this class. She comes in late almost every day and is always disruptive during class periods. Does not ask to use restroom, just leaves class whenever she

wants to. Consistently talks over me to fellow classmates who are trying to listen…

Ha! Someone had no self-awareness.

…spends most of her trusted computer time surfing the web, and relentlessly tries to entertain the class by being inappropriate and disrespectful…

I stopped reading. He was obviously making me out to be an awful, desperate class clown, and I didn't need to read anymore of that nonsense. I ripped the letter in half, and then, considering the embarrassment if someone were to read it, ripped it a few more times before tossing it in the nearest trash can.

Why was he foolish enough to think I would actually bring it with me?

IN THE MAIN OFFICE, I decided to tell the secretary that I would "like to speak with Headmaster Ransic" rather than say "I was made to come here due to my frequent tardiness and disregard for rules."

She smiled, indicated that I should sit in one of the seats around the corner from her and said she'd call me when the headmaster was ready to see me.

I turned the corner and took a second to consider

my options. I could sit next to this kid, Vince, who seemed to be there every time I was and who always tried to make conversation with me that was riddled with clichés, like "What're y'in for?" and who muttered things like "Pissin' contest." He was a textbook bully and had been taking lunch money from kids for years, which only made him more irritating.

I found him loathsome, exactly the kind of low-rent person I hated. It's like he thought it his duty to make other people's lives harder for no reason at all. This was like his third year as a senior, and he seemed to look more disgusting and unwashed every day. But I suppose that made sense, if he didn't bathe.

And it smelled like he didn't.

I could sit next to Brett, who was probably there to talk about picking up some more community service hours or something equally academically-oriented to help him get into college, where he seemed so desperate to go, to make up for his years as a rebel.

Or I could sit next to a girl I remembered from my first class on my first day in high school.

The teacher of that class had not had either of our names on the roll, and had asked for anyone who hadn't heard their name to raise their hand. We were sitting next to each other, and when we both raised our hands she had leaned toward me to say, "God, we're such losers, aren't we?" and laughed nervously.

I remember observing her low ponytail, too-light-and-shiny lipgloss and under-plucked eyebrows, and thinking, *Well, one of us is,* and not responding to her.

From what I had seen of her in the last few years, she seemed just as frantic for camaraderie and as ill-advised fashion-wise as she was then.

I took a seat next to Brett, guessing that he was the most likely to stay silent.

I was wrong. And I should have known better. He'd been trying to talk to me recently.

"Hey, Bridget." He waved as he said it. Why wave? Like I'd wonder where on earth that voice was coming from if he didn't?

I pulled my lips tight, making an expression that barely passed as a smile. It was impolite, but I wasn't in the mood to make small talk.

He didn't say anything else as we sat there, which was a long time, since the other two were called into the headmaster's office first. When Brett's name was called, he leapt from his seat like a cartoon character and walked as fast as he could without running.

Once he'd left, I went back to reading the magazine I'd stashed in my Prada bag.

Finally I heard my name called in the secretary's nasally voice, and I headed toward the headmaster's office. I noticed that Brett, who was exiting, avoided eye contact with me.

Drama queen.

By the time I reached the door of the office, I had plastered a wide smile across my face, all thoughts of Brett out the window. I shut the door behind me.

"Good morning, Headmaster." I acted like we were old friends meeting for lunch. "You're pretty busy for so early in the morning." I pointed a polished finger toward the now-empty waiting area.

"Yes, well, I've only got these seven and a half hours to fit in all the angst of private high school. So what is it you're here for, Miss Duke?"

I let my smile fade and traded it for a much more serious expression, as I prepared to get out of trouble. My charm was a useful tool in these situations.

"Well—" I began, and the phone on his desk rang. He excused himself and answered it. I studied him as he listened to the person on the other line.

Headmaster Ransic was probably in his late forties and had obviously been attractive in his younger years. His hair was a little thin and graying at the temples, and there were faint lines in his face when he spoke or smiled, but he had blue eyes in a shade that looked hot on younger guys. There was something about him that made it seem strange that he worked at a school.

Perhaps it was his unkempt way of dressing and doing (or not doing) his hair. He seemed perfectly competent, but the fact that he wasn't a carbon copy of some musty old politician seemed to turn off most of the parents at the school.

His desk, too, was different than the usual kind. It had none of those silly metal toys or anything. He had a frame that pictured him and a pretty woman who, judging by his naked ring finger, was his girlfriend. He had a couple of things that I supposed could only be called artifacts: one rock with two faces carved into it, a bowl that looked handmade and ancient and a few wooden sculptures. The only thing on the desk that looked at all academic or work-related was the yellow legal pad that lay in front of him.

I was just tilting my head to see what was written on the pad when he said, "All right then, I'll talk to you later, John," and hung up. I jerked guiltily back into a normal non-nosy position.

"All right, surprise me." He leaned back in his chair.

From his knowing tone, I could tell that the jig was

up. I was going to have to come up with a plan to get out of trouble. One that could explain my constant lateness and perhaps score me the chance to continue with my habit of sleeping in a bit.

"Well…it's kind of hard to talk about."

Probably because I didn't know what I was going to say.

"It's an easy question. Why is it that you can't make it to class on time, like every other student?"

I took a deep breath. "It's my parents. Well, it's my stepmother. I've hardly been able to get any sleep at home lately, so getting up so early has been a…" I searched for the right word "…challenge."

"And why is that?"

Because I was watching reality TV late into the night and ignoring the texts of needy girls asking me to come hang out and guys asking *Hey, what are you up to tonight?*

"Well…" I tried to come up with something so personal that he wouldn't dare pursue the subject. Maybe refer me to the guidance office, so I could get the hell out of here.

"Yes…?"

"Well, when my dad's there, there's a lot of yelling." At the Redskins, the Orioles and every other sports team he followed like a maniac. I contemplated my next implication. "And when he's not, there are other noises."

"Other *noises?*"

I bit my lip and looked down for a moment before meeting his eyes and delivering what I hoped would be The Silencer.

"My stepmother has…guests. Well, one guy in particular. It's…uncomfortable to be around at those times especially, but—" I shrugged "—you know."

My implication hung in the air for a moment, before he finally had the decency to look embarrassed and avert his eyes.

The truth was, the only objectionable sounds I'd ever heard coming from my stepmother's room when my father was away were strains of Rod Stewart albums and, on one memorable occasion, the Partridge Family. And, more embarrassingly, her thin voice singing along.

But the headmaster didn't know that.

The closest thing Meredith had to a male guest was Todd, the flaming interior decorator she'd employed for years who kept trying to leave chintz throw pillows on my bed. Apparently the mess in my room was "insulting" to him.

But the headmaster didn't know that either.

"Really." He didn't say it like he wanted an answer. So I kept talking.

"Um, yeah. I mean I have to see him like five days a week, you know? That's what makes it even worse." I tried to look tortured for a moment. It was true; Todd was there all the time. Since Meredith didn't have a job, she had nothing better to do than to redecorate every room in my house from bottom to top, baseboard to crown molding. I also suspected Todd might be one of her best friends.

I wasn't sure if that was sad or not.

"That must be difficult," he agreed, looking hesitant.

I nodded. Now it was time to get back on track.

"Listen, I'm not really comfortable talking about this," I said, and it was true. "The point is that I think it's been hard at home, and it's been hard in class."

He paused. "I certainly am sorry to hear about your trouble at home, but I still don't see what one has to do with the other."

Why wasn't he letting this *go?*

I floundered, trying to wrap it up in a way that made sense.

"Well, how would you like to have the two people who hate you most *plotting* together about your future for their own convenience?" I was embarrassed at how clear the hurt was in my voice.

But Mr. Ransic had already lost patience. "Miss Duke, I still don't see what you're talking about, and the point—"

"What I'm *talking about* is my stepmother and Mr. Ezhno's little private…'rendezvous.'" I was raising my voice a little bit more, not having realized how mad I was about this until now. All the parent-teacher conferences that Meredith left saying what a "nice man" Mr. Ezhno was, and how "we both" just want the best for me, and that this kind of behavior wouldn't "cut it in college."

"I mean, why should I have to suffer because my teacher is, like, in love with my stepmom and he's trying to impress her or whatever by scheming with her?"

I was practically panting.

"Are you saying—"

"I'm saying it's *personal,*" I spat. "*Not* professional. Not *academic. Per-son-al.*"

Mr. Ransic finally looked like he didn't know what to say. Thank *God.* It was about time he pulled his nose out of my business. Whether it was imaginary business or not.

At last, looking as if he had a speculative grasp on the

situation and the fact that Mr. Ezhno and Meredith had something personal against me and that I needed help, not punishment, he said something about his busy day and stood up to open the door for me. I walked out, finally free from being judged.

TWO HOURS LATER, I WAS in the locker room with Michelle, one of my best friends. Our gym lockers were next to one another, which was convenient for my venting.

"I was *seriously* only thirty seconds late. And it wasn't even my fault! It was his be*loved* Meredith's fault."

"Yeah, that sucks." Michelle pulled on her shorts. She'd had them since freshman year, and they didn't really fit her anymore.

"You know, you should really buy new shorts this year. Those are getting a little tight on your hips. I think they'll order some for you if they don't have your size."

I pulled on mine, which I'd been forced to buy two sizes too big because I got stuck with one of the last pairs before I knew they could just order them, and my father had told me to deal with them (his go-to response whenever I complained—it really sucks that he's not a pushover). Meredith had said, in that irritatingly sweet way of hers, that maybe I'd grow into them. Yeah, right, like I'd ever let myself go up *two* sizes.

They were constantly slipping down, putting me an inch away from embarrassment every time. "Mine, on the other hand, are huge." I pulled on the waist-band, and looked down at my sneakers through the pant legs.

"Okay, so what happened when you came in late?" Michelle asked sharply.

"Basically, he sent me to the office with this totally stupid note talking about how I'm some kind of menace. Ugh, and he said something about me distracting other students who were *trying to pay attention.*"

I watched Michelle for an aghast reaction, and was disappointed to see her fiddling with the cord on her shorts.

I kept talking. "It was so stupid. So then I had to wait for like, ever, with three of Winchester Prep's Least Wanted." I looked expectantly at Michelle again.

She was tugging violently on her waistband now.

"Are you even listening, Michelle? Or are you just going to rip your pants trying to make them fit?"

She looked up, like she'd forgotten I was there.

"Oh, sorry, go on, I was listening."

I sighed. "So, finally I go in, right, and then I'm about to be super-nice and just say something about how I promised not to be late anymore, and how homework's been hard lately, possibly start crying, and then..." I paused for emphasis "...Mr. Ezhno actually *called* the office to tell him that not only was I late but that I was disruptive or whatever."

"Seriously?"

"Seriously. So then I knew I was going to have to think fast, and really all I wanted to do was to get out of there, right? So I start talking about how Meredith's always got this 'male guest' over."

Michelle didn't see my finger quotes, or my self-impressed smile, because she was back to messing with her shorts.

My smile faded and I decided to finish my story, because *obviously* she was incapable of paying attention. "I just complained about how she and Mr. Ezhno were always meeting and stuff, and how he was like in *love* with her, and how everything he does is because of that." I looked at her. Was *nothing* I said going to get her attention? "And how they're totally doing it," I added, just to get a reaction.

"Wait, what?" She looked up.

I glared at her, and a whistle blew to indicate the beginning of gym. Oblivious to the ball I'd just set rolling, I flounced off to class.

# CHAPTER TWO

The next day, I showed up to Mr. Ezhno's class on time. Frankly, it wasn't in reaction to his threat of suspension, but more just needing to escape my house and Meredith's sobbing. If I didn't hate her so much, I might have asked her what was wrong. I couldn't stand it when other people cried around me. I always felt guilty, even when I hadn't done anything wrong.

But seriously, who wakes up at seven o'clock in the morning to cry?

As soon as I sat down, Jillian, my other, more gossip-appreciating best friend, passed me a neatly folded note (she'd been the first one in fourth grade to be able to make origami and paper footballs).

I looked up at her. "You can't just say it? We have to pass notes?"

It sounded kind of mean, but come on, everyone was talking and class hadn't even started yet.

Jillian made a face and mouthed, "Just read it."

I opened the note and started to read the rounded, funky handwriting I'd never been able to copy. Instead, I had total boy handwriting.

*Michelle told me about everything that you told her about Mr. Ezhno. Is it true?*

I nodded and made a gagging face. Her eyes widened, along with her mouth. *Finally* someone appreciated how irritating the situation was. I felt a wave of fondness for Jillian, as I saw how commiserative she was.

As class started, I wrote back, asking her what else had been going on in school. She had some decent gossip, as usual. It was really the main reason I kept her around. Jillian had an amazing ability to remember just about everything. She didn't use her memory to score high on tests and do well in Spanish class—obviously, if she was talking to me all through class, she couldn't hear that information to memorize it. She used her memory exclusively to collect and archive everything about everyone we went to school with.

Jillian was going on about the colleges everyone was

interested in applying to, and the boy who'd just gotten kicked off the soccer team for having a 1.9 GPA. I had just been about to say something about "getting to the good stuff" when she mentioned that there was a new girl.

"...1.9 GPA, which is so sad, because it's only like point-*one* away from being acceptable. Oh! And that new girl is in my gym class, speaking of soccer. She was actually really good."

I thought of Liam and the girl I hadn't recognized the day before. "So, wait, did you talk to her?"

"Oh, yeah, she's *so* nice. Her name is Anna Judge, and she moved here from Maine. It's actually kind of funny, I kept running into her and Liam yesterday. Seriously, like, all day."

My opportunity. "Liam?"

I spoke too quickly. Super casual. But thankfully, Jillian never noticed that kind of thing and simply answered my question.

"Oh, right, he was showing her around yesterday. You know how the office, like, assigns you a buddy or whatever on your first day when you're new?"

"Yeah, go on."

*SPIT. IT. OUT.*

"Well, Liam was her buddy. I mean, he was assigned

to do it, but I *heard* he volunteered. He was apparently in the office picking up some form for football when she came in. He dropped her off at each class, picked her up, ate lunch with her, all that normal stuff that the buddy guides do—"

Or all that stuff that he used to do with me every single day.

"—except he drove her home, too, which they don't always do."

No, they didn't.

They *never* did that.

I spent the rest of the period prodding her for information about Liam and Anna. She spoke delicately, in accordance to my sensitivity on the subject of him. My best friends knew it was a hot button for me. But once she told me she didn't know anything else, I knew she was telling the truth. Jillian was honest, always. Which was the reason she was the wrong person to tell a secret to, but an excellent person to leak them from.

She did keep talking about how super-nice Anna had been.

Not so delicate.

When the bell finally rang, I was more than ready to leave. I was the first one out the door, tossing an "Oh, bye!" back to Jillian. I had thought that getting out of the classroom and away from Jillian would be enough to relieve me of having to think about the new girl and her friendship (or whatever it might become) with Liam. But as I walked down the hallway, it seemed like her name was on everyone's lips. Maybe it was all in my head, but even if it was, it was pissing me off.

I ducked into the bathroom, hoping to renew my self-confidence with the reapplication of lipgloss. And there she was.

Miss Anna Judge, the Super-Nice, Surprisingly-Good-Soccer-Player from Maine. Washing what looked like ink from her fingers.

What could be more awkward for me than to stand elbow to elbow with the girl who I had only seen from a hundred yards away but had already devoted so much thought to? Not awkward for her, of course; she didn't even know who I was.

Oh, my God, she didn't even know who I *was*.

I felt the petty, obsessive, desperate-to-be-liked feeling that had been living in my stomach since I was in elementary school. That was always ready to jump out and whine, *But what about me?* Whenever I felt it, I'd usually try to say or do something to draw the attention to myself.

And keep it there.

I walked to the other sink, next to her, and started to dig through my bag for my NARS lipgloss.

There was no one at the school who *didn't* know who I was. I'd worked hard to make it that way. At this point, half the guys were trying to get with me, and half the girls were jealous of that fact or trying just as hard to be part of my inner circle.

I had parties all the time, and everyone knew I only invited the people I wanted to. It didn't hurt that I had the best pool in Potomac Falls.

Though my dad and Meredith were strictly against alcohol at the parties, we usually managed to spike the punch. Then we'd just claim it was a slumber party, and *that's* why no one drove home 'til morning. Meredith would spend days planning the decorations, themed music, (temporarily) virgin drinks and anything else she or I could think of. It was pretty cool of her—not that I could ever get over my issues with her enough to tell her so.

It was even cooler that she would then spend the whole time in her room or out with my father, out of our way.

I redirected my thoughts back to figuring why Anna simply *must* know whom she was standing next to. Surely she'd heard someone talk about me, or something. Maybe someone had pointed me out to her while I was too busy to notice. I pulled out the lipgloss and started applying it, still considering other probable reasons why she simply must know who I was. She was just *pretending* not to.

I risked a glance at her reflection.

She had short, silvery-blond hair, which seemed to me like an obvious effort to look spunky and fun. She had long eyelashes, and the smooth skin I had always assured myself was just airbrushing in magazines and pictures of celebrities. Her arms were thin, just like the rest of her. She was wearing a dress that was bound to be "in" soon. She was still scrubbing her hands.

Then she spoke, taking me off guard. It was like I'd forgotten she could see me, too.

"Pen exploded. I didn't kill a squid or anything." She smiled, exposing straight, white teeth. "I'm Anna, by the way."

I nodded curtly and smiled back. "Hi, Anna."

I didn't tell her who I was. I had to see if she already knew. *Had* to.

"And you are…Bridget Duke?"

My mind eased. What had I been worried about?

"Yes, I am." I waited a moment before deciding that, yes, I needed validation. "How did you know that?"

"Oh, sorry, that must seem creepy. I saw the name on the corner of the paper sticking out of your bag. I'm new here."

I paused as the disappointment set in.

"Okay, then." I turned back to my mirror and started fussing over my eye makeup.

I tried desperately to think of something cool to say while she nonchalantly applied ChapStick to her lips (which didn't seem to need it).

"Actually," Anna started, still not looking at me, "I think Liam mentioned your name. Do you know Liam?"

I mused over the simplicity of the question, and the understatement that would be my answer.

"Yes, I know him."

"Hmm. He told me to look out for you."

She glanced at me, smiled again and waved goodbye.

My face was frozen in shock as I stared at the doorway until she was gone and her footsteps faded. It felt like she'd just pulled the pin out of a grenade, and I had no idea how to stop it from exploding.

I LEFT THE BATHROOM—the scene of the crime—in a daze.

I was analyzing, picking at and utterly disassembling

what Anna had told me Liam had said. I'd done this many times with things he'd said to me, each time shredding his words so thoroughly that I worked myself into a fit. Sure, this was she-said he-said, but it didn't matter. Liam said a lot of cryptic things, seemingly not on purpose.

I'd particularly agonized over what he'd said when he broke up with me. He'd said that of course it wasn't what he wanted, and that maybe sometime in the future…

Oh, he'd given me plenty to mull over that night.

So, there I was, putting on the familiar thinking cap specifically designed for figuring out what the *hell* Liam meant by what he said.

*He told me to look out for you.*

Because she should get to know me, or because I am someone to avoid?

I decided I would definitely have to use one of my other favorite techniques: bringing Liam up into every single conversation and asking what everyone else thought he might have meant.

I had just decided to go to the nurse's office because of imaginary cramps and say that I was really not able to stay the rest of the day when Brett popped up out of nowhere.

"Hey, Bridget—ready for this test in NSL?"

I always hated small talk about classes, particularly National, State and Local Government. *Blech.*

"Ugh, Brett, what are you—" Wait. "What test?"

"What *test?*" He repeated my words with an entirely different inflection, one that implied that I was very, very stupid. "The midterm, Bridget. You studied for it, right?"

"No? When is it?"

"Today, in like—" he looked at his watch—which, incidentally, looked like it was taken from the personal wardrobe of Inspector Gadget "—forty-six minutes."

He was still looking horrified at my unpreparedness.

"How much is it worth?" I asked, feeling a little breathless. *Today sucks,* I thought.

"Thirty percent, just like the final, and then the other forty percent is homework and the other quizzes and stuff."

Oh, no. I had gotten a D on the last quiz and forgotten about three homework assignments. On last week's progress report I'd had a seventy-two percent in the class. I had to pass.

"Brett, there's no way I can study enough during this

lunch period. You have to help me." I said this last part like it was obvious.

"I can't help you study, Bridget, I have no time—"

"No, not study, *Brett,* you have to help me during the test."

Technically, I was asking for a favor and, really, one shouldn't treat the person she wants a favor from like he's stupid. But Brett didn't seem to notice. His expression just turned from worry for me to worry for himself.

He understood exactly what I was saying. "I can't, Bridget. If we got caught, I'd fail this test, then my grade would drop down to a sixty-six percent. I have to work really hard to keep my grades high enough to get into college." He shook his head. "There's no way."

"Oh, my God, we're not going to get caught." I had no idea if we'd get caught, but I tried to sound confident. "This'll be so simple, she'll never notice. Okay, are you right-handed?"

"Yes?"

"Okay, then you sit to my left, and I'll sit behind Walco, he's huge, Mrs. Remeley won't be able to see me look at your paper. All you have to do is write really clearly and keep your paper diagonal toward me. It'll be no problem, it's how most people write, anyway."

He looked firm on his refusal. And then the obvious struck me.

"Michelle. I'll trade you Michelle!" I said it like I'd figured out the Da Vinci Code or something.

Brett had had a totally annoying crush on Michelle since, like, first grade. She and I hadn't really been friends yet at that age, but my mom knew her mom, so we played with each other. She used to get secret-admirer cards and letters. A fact I teased her about because I was positively green with envy, and resentful that no one sent any to me. Except for that one I'd written to myself once, and claimed it was from resident cutie J.R.

We didn't know for sure who was writing them to her until one day in fifth grade, when I caught Brett in the cubby room writing one while everyone else was playing Heads Up Seven Up. I'd been cold and going to get my jacket when I found him.

There he was, sitting in the corner with a piece of pink construction paper on his lap, writing in the boyish handwriting I recognized from all the other valentines over the years.

Lying on the floor next to him were several failed attempts. I remember the validation of my suspicions that it was he who had been writing them feeling like a victory.

Snatching the card from his lap, I ran out of the cubby room shouting "Brett loves Miche-elle" in that singsong voice strictly used in this particular brand of torture. Everyone's head had shot up, and I read the poem aloud.

Though my love goes unrequited
I'll love you beyond when the pigs are flighted.
Though I may be a snowball, and you the heat
I'll melt with you if you stay as sweet.
You are Michelle, my belle,
And without you, this place would be…

Brett would later insist that he hadn't intended to put *hell* at the end of the poem, but was going to somehow rhyme *dwell*. But to us, it might as well have been written there.

None of us knew the real meanings behind the words. Even so, the class got what the poem meant: it meant that Brett wanted to be K-I-S-S-I-N-G Michelle. Sitting in a tree, if you went by our prediction.

Brett had stayed in the cubby room the entire time I read it, and the only other person, besides him and our dimwitted teacher, not joining in the roar of laughter was Michelle. She had turned a deep shade of red and then run to the bathroom. Brett went to the office and got picked up early that day.

All the while, our teacher handed out bags of heart-shaped candies, an uncomprehending smile on her face.

A few years later, when we all entered middle school, Brett had come in with a seriously misguided attempt at dyed black hair, which had come out a sort of awful, metallic blue, and a newfound interest in all things rebellious. He didn't start dressing normally again (i.e., not wearing the goth-style pants that looked like an entire flap of a circus tent had been stitched together) and stop skipping school until tenth grade. That was also when he started obsessing about the grades he couldn't seem to keep up very easily.

Judging by the way Brett never spoke to Michelle again and instead gazed at her every chance he got, I was pretty sure he still wanted to sit in a tree with her. Lucky for me, his expression when I said her name removed all doubt from my mind.

"What about Michelle? What do you mean you'll trade her?"

"I'll get you a date with her if you give me the answers."

He hesitated. I saw something that looked like the tiniest bit of consideration in his eyes. I jumped at it.

"Come on, Brett, it's totally worth it. It's not like we'll get caught. And, be real, when else are you going to have a chance with Michelle?" He looked a little offended and, for some reason I could not imagine, amused.

I would have felt bad saying that he didn't have a shot with her except that it was true. And just because I pointed out the obvious didn't mean it was my fault that he never would have asked her out.

"It's not right, you can't expect to just trade her like money or something." He seemed to give himself an idea. "Here, just ask her to talk to me. I'll ask her out myself."

Ha! He was making this way too easy.

"So we have a deal." It wasn't a question. I wanted him to feel like he had already agreed. "She'll sit with you Monday at lunch."

I snickered to myself and walked past him to the

cafeteria. But as soon as I walked away, Liam loomed in my mind again, removing any trace of laughter.

I STAYED QUIET THROUGHOUT the lunch period, ignoring the gossip Jillian was imparting to Michelle. Instead of participating, I spent the whole period looking through my *Allure* magazine and glancing at Liam as furtively and often as possible.

He was about six foot three, his body lean and toned. His hair was the dark, shiny brown that you might see in a shampoo commercial, and reached down just past his dark, straight eyebrows. His eyes, though I couldn't see them from where I sat, I knew to be the same light color of a swimming pool. The dark circle of his pupil and his thick, dark, straight eyelashes made the color seem even more striking.

He was sitting with Anna, who was taking a bite out of a cheeseburger. Eyeing the bottle of Coke Classic that sat in front of her, I wondered how she ate like that and still stayed so thin. Even if we *had* been friends, though, I never would have asked her that—that was what people asked *me.*

Not the other way around.

I decided that of all things, I didn't have the energy to look at the pair of them.

"Bridget?"

I blinked away images of times Liam's eyes had been close enough to mine that I could memorize them.

"What?" I snapped, and looked up to see a girl named Laura's eager-looking face.

She recoiled slightly at the harshness in my tone. "Um. Well, I was, uh…" she nervously tripped over her words "…wondering if you guys wanted to come over to my house tonight. I mean, it's not going to be like a big deal party or anything. Not like *your* parties."

"Have you ever actually *been* to one of my parties?" I asked impatiently, barely interested in the conversation.

"Um. No, but, I mean, I hear they're great."

I narrowed my eyes at her and cocked my head a bit to the side. She cleared her throat.

"Well, anyway, it's just going to be like board games and stuff. My parents will be there." She looked sheepish.

I waited to see if she said anything else. When she didn't, and instead shifted her weight uncomfortably, I smiled.

"Uh-huh. Well, I know that I'll be busy tonight. I don't know about the other girls. Michelle? Jillian? Busy tonight? Want to go play some board games with Laura and her parents?"

Michelle shook her head down at her food, her face red. Jillian looked sympathetically at Laura and then said something about plans with her mom.

I crinkled my nose, and made a tsk-ing sound as I turned back to Laura looking regretful.

"Aw, that's too bad. Maybe next time?" I smiled dismissively, and looked back down at my magazine.

"You know what, Bridget?" Laura asked, her ears turning red.

I gave her a challenging look. "What's that?"

"You're just..."

There was a lurch in my stomach. I would not be told off, and I could tell that was where this was going. But I'd learned long ago to deflect this sort of thing. "I'd stop now, if I were you. Which thank *God* I'm not."

I watched her fury grow, and I felt the growing sense that I'd really gone too far.

"I'd always rather be me than you." And she walked away.

I scrambled to think of something to say. I thought of nothing. I'd never *had* to. Since when did anyone challenge me?

I knew I'd been unnecessarily cruel to her, and I felt

kind of guilty. But my day had sucked so far, too, and no one was apologizing to *me*.

"Bridget—"

"So I ran into Anna today," I started, cutting off Michelle. I knew she was going to give me grief and I just couldn't deal with *that* on top of it all. Plus, I had to pretend that what had just happened didn't bother me. "And she introduced herself to me and all—she already knew my name—and then told me that Liam had told her to 'look out for' me. What do you suppose that means?"

Jillian, always interested in a good outrage, gasped and dropped her celery stick. "He said that?"

I enlightened her on my theories of what he might have meant, and we talked about it for the rest of the period, eventually agreeing that he must have meant that I am so popular she's bound to run into me, and to then introduce herself.

As soon as the bell rang indicating the end of lunch, I told Michelle about the deal I'd made with Brett. Well, I told her the half she needed to know, which was that she was sitting with him on Monday at lunch.

She raised her eyebrows at me.

"I'm *what?*"

"It's no big deal. Seriously, I said I'd get him a date,

and all he wanted was to ask you out himself." She stared at me. "Oh, my God, Michelle, just say no to him, it's not that hard."

"Bridget, you can't just—"

What, now *she* was going to start rebelling, too?

"Well, you're going to sit with him, so…" I let the *so* hang in the air, letting her fill in the blank for herself with *stop arguing with me.* I smiled superficially, wiggled a goodbye with my fingers to Jillian and then strutted off to class. I didn't look back to see what Michelle did next.

As I walked away, I began to wonder if what I was about to do was wrong. Sure, chances were that Brett wouldn't get caught helping me, and that he wouldn't dive into a depression when Michelle said no to his date. But still—what if we did get caught? What if he did fail the class, and it was my fault? What if between that and Michelle rejecting him, he did slip into a depression? Anyone would, after being expelled from this school. It was such a high-profile place that anything that happened here was practically in the society pages.

But no, I thought to myself. I was giving my actions far more credit than they deserved. Brett would be fine. We wouldn't get caught, and even if we did… Brett would be fine.

My conviction wavered a bit once I walked into my NSL class and saw that there was a substitute teacher.

Okay, this could go one of two ways. Either the sub was nicer than Mrs. Remeley, our usual teacher, or she could be nasty.

Nasty like that teacher we'd had in middle school who kept telling us to sit up straight and hold our books a certain way during reading time.

Nice like my first grade teacher with Valentine's Day candy and the inability to stop me from doing what I wanted. Which, in first grade, was to use Brett to my advantage.

On my way to my seat, I watched her. She looked to be about in her fifties, but according to the chalkboard, she was a "Miss." Miss Smithson. She was mousy and looked nervous. I instantly felt some indefinable emotion for her.

Brett was in his seat looking down at his notes when I sat down. I tapped him on the shoulder.

"Hey, Brett?"

"Yeah?" he asked, eyes still on his paper. I clicked my tongue at his lack of interest in what I had to say.

"I talked to Michelle." I grinned as he looked up at me. "She's looking forward to Monday."

I could tell that he wasn't sure if I was telling the truth

or not. Whatever, he was probably hopeful enough to choose to believe I was telling the truth. And there was nothing wrong with giving him some hope. Especially because my hope was that this encouragement would stop him from backing out.

The bell rang, and Miss Smithson cleared her throat.

"Good afternoon, students!" She waited for a response. Though she didn't seem to notice, the only response she got was a raised eyebrow from me. "As you know, you've got a test today. It's only three pages long, and it's all multiple-choice. I'm sure you'll all do fine."

*Really, you are?* I thought, unnecessarily.

She started passing out the papers.

"Be sure to write your names in the upper right-hand corner!"

This spurt of enthusiasm had me raising both of my eyebrows.

When the test finally got to me, I wrote my name and took a look at the first question.

What the hell was "gerrymandering"?

I looked over at Brett's paper, which already bore the answers to three questions on the first page. I circled the *a* on the first question and hurried to write the other answers. He couldn't go this fast, or I wouldn't keep up.

"*Slow down!*" I commanded in a whisper out of the side of my mouth.

He looked at me, looked at the substitute and then ripped the corner off of the first page of his test. The teacher looked up, and we both tried to look busy. She finally put her nose back into her romance novel, and I glared at Brett.

I inhaled deeply as I saw that he was writing something to me in his slanted handwriting, which gave all of his letters long stems.

He slid the note onto my desk. After one glare at him for his entire lack of stealth and several discreet glances at the teacher, I opened the note and read it.

*I can't do this. You have to do the work.*

My eyes and mouth widened and I turned toward Brett, who was staring determinedly down at his paper. What was *happening* to everyone? No one ever said no to me!

I spoke through my teeth. *"You. Have. To."*

"I can't," he whispered. "I can't risk it."

Out of the corner of my eye, I saw Miss Smithson stand up and walk toward us. I shushed Brett, who was no longer making any noise, and went back to my test.

My heart was beating so hard, I was sure she would see the pounding in my chest. I circled the other answers that Brett had put down and answered the two following without reading the questions. I heard her soft, non-heeled steps come closer and finally stop in front of our desks.

"Could you two please step out into the hall?"

There were times when I was trying to get away with something but felt positive that the fact that I was practically swallowing my face would give me away.

This was one of those times.

How was this possible? Out of absolutely *nowhere,* everything I did today was failing. Nothing was going my way. And truthfully? That's not how my life works.

I looked up to see Brett's panicked glare and then Miss Smithson's disappointed gaze. We walked out into the echoing hall and she followed us. Once in the hall, she headed for the staff lounge a few doors down.

Brett and I stood in silence for a few seconds.

"I, um…" I wasn't sure what I was going to say, whether it would come out as an apology or as an accusation. I didn't have time to decide because, at that moment, Miss Smithson came out of the lounge. Chubby little Ms. Chase, whose mouth was full of food and who had clearly just been pulled from her lunch period, followed.

Ms. Chase waved jovially at Brett and me, and then walked into the NSL classroom to chaperone. To make sure no one else was cheating, I guess.

What was I going to do if my father found out about this? He was no tyrant, but he would definitely find cheating unacceptable. There would be angry words. Punishment. Disappointment. Though that might be my own, once Meredith was proven right about me. That I could not handle.

When I had done something wrong was the *only* time I was even a little not-horribly-resentful that my mother had died in a car accident when I was seven. That way I had only one parent I worried about, one stepparent I couldn't care less about and one parent I tried never to think about.

I was so busy worrying about what my father was going to say when he found out that when Miss Smithson spoke, I was surprised.

"Cheating," she said, looking far more intimidating than I had initially suspected, "is an unacceptable act of behavior. I must say I am disappointed."

I thought nastily of asking her how in the world she

could be disappointed in us when she didn't know us to begin with.

She continued on. "Now which one of you wants to explain to me what happened?"

If I had been a cartoon character, there would have been an exclamation point over my head.

She wanted *one of us* to explain.

She didn't know which one of us had done the cheating. I wasn't dead, not yet. My next words came tumbling from my mouth faster than I could think them through.

"I tried to tell him to stop, Miss Smithson. I know it's wrong to talk during a test, but I didn't know what else to do." I looked her in the eyes, and tried to look as sincere as possible. "I'm so sorry, Miss Smithson, really."

I knew it was wrong to cheat. I knew it was wrong to lie. I knew it was wrong to push someone in front of a speeding train. But all I could think at that moment was that I had to get out of trouble.

And somehow, miraculously, it looked like I might.

"Brett, is this true?" Miss Smithson's gaze shifted to him. I could feel his eyes on me.

"I was trying to tell *her* not to cheat!" The pure rage in his voice shook me.

Miss Smithson had seen it all before. "You're either going to agree here on who it was, or you're both going to be punished to the full extent." She watched us, waiting for one of us to say something.

"I understand," I said. One of the things I understood was that Brett was going to get in trouble for something he didn't do. I knew that I would probably be in the same amount of trouble either way, and that I was dragging Brett down with me. I also knew that this was the perfect chance to tell the truth.

But I couldn't do it. I don't know why.

And then I made it all worse by remembering the note Brett had passed me. I pulled it out of my pocket and handed it to Miss Smithson.

"See? You can see that it's his, because it's the corner of the first page on his test." It was from him. The words were his. The meaning, however, had shifted to suit me. "See, he said he couldn't do it, and that *I* had to do the work. For him."

Miss Smithson took the piece of paper from my outstretched hand. Lifting her glasses from the chain that hung them around her neck, she read it.

"Did you write this?" she asked Brett, peering at him

over the top rims of her lenses, which were scooted down her nose.

I was banking on him starting with the truth.

He did.

"Yes, but—" Brett said, desperately trying to explain what I had done. It was too late.

"All right then," she finally said, "gather your things and go to the office. Miss Duke, I know it doesn't feel like you've done anything wrong, but you'll have to go explain what happened to the headmaster. I'll call to let him know you're coming."

On the way to the office, I kept my face pointed purposefully in front of me, terrified to make eye contact with Brett. Not that I would have if I had looked at him, because he wouldn't look at me either. I didn't blame him; he must have been disgusted with me. I wanted to fix it, but it was too late. If I said something now, I'd be in even more trouble.

Trouble I couldn't afford. And something in me knew that I would never have chosen to be noble and do the right thing. There was no taking it back. I always took the self-preservation route.

But maybe I could explain to Brett why I *really* couldn't get in trouble right now. Last time I'd gotten in trouble, my father had given me this death stare he's awesome at, and told me that I didn't even want to know how much things would change if I got in trouble again at school.

"Listen, Brett—"

"Shut up, Bridget."

I gasped and resolved to stick to my lie when I spoke to the headmaster. Perhaps even make up some more lies.

# CHAPTER THREE

I spent the afternoon trying to forget how awful school had been for the past two days. I tried to forget the meeting in the office about Mr. Ezhno, the conversation with Anna, the test, the consequent *second* meeting in the office and seeing Liam with Anna *everywhere.*

They never looked romantic, but that didn't mean they wouldn't be. I knew Liam to be the perfect gentleman, one who would be very cautious not to rush things. Ever again, anyway.

The second meeting with Headmaster Ransic had been awful. It was like I was hypnotized into lying again and again.

Of course, I was not hypnotized, and didn't have the luxury of having that as an excuse. I was just watching my own back and no one else's. I had spoken to Headmaster Ransic before Brett, given my story—and it *was* a story—and agreed that it was true, things really weren't going my way lately. I then walked out of the office, trying hard not to look anyone in the eyes. I left feeling like if I did catch anyone's glance, I was sure to be found out. And then, instead of being given any mercy for ultimately telling the truth, I'd get in trouble for the whole thing. I wasn't exactly on death row, but still. Being expelled from Winchester Prep and not going to college would have been mortifying. Unheard of.

The talk of the town. Especially if it was because of something stupid like this.

I decided I shouldn't think about it too hard. So after figuring that spending most of an afternoon by myself was enough coping, I decided it was time to move on to bitching.

And that meant calling Jillian and Michelle to come over for Chinese food and, though I didn't mention it, a bitch-fest.

Michelle said she'd come over, but after dinner. Jillian was all for it, and said she'd be over as soon as she could. I told her to pick up the Chinese, and that it should be on her. I reminded her that she owed me for the pair of Von Dutch jeans I'd given her anyway. I'd given them to her because my father had made some comment about them being tight, and since then I had felt self-conscious in them. Not that I'd admit that. I just told her that I'd never liked them.

When Jillian finally got there, we settled onto the couch with our chopsticks and paper boxes of food and turned on some trashy reality TV show.

I took a bite of my chicken fried rice and glanced at her. She looked down, dipped her dumpling in soy sauce and took a bite. I contained myself for a few minutes as we ate our food and watched the show. Then I launched into what had happened with Brett.

Well, the version of the story she had to hear. That was the biggest problem with Jillian; every word I said to her had to be carefully considered, as if I was shouting it through a megaphone.

It's not that Jillian went around whispering other people's secrets into people's ears like in that old Norman Rockwell painting. She just let everyone in on the secrets through heavy implications, broad hints and, from the experience I had with extracting the best gossip from her, a lot of facial expressions that served as answers to leading questions. I truly believed, however, that she didn't do it intentionally. You could doubtless hook her up to a lie detector and she would pass with flying colors.

She honestly seemed unaware.

So that was why I was going to have to be careful what I said to her.

"Okay, so are you ready to the hear about the biggest drama of this week?"

"Um, duh?"

I told her everything I had told Headmaster Ransic. Everything from how *hard* I'd studied to Brett passing me the note during class, to getting caught, feeling bad about having to rat out Brett and going to the office. She drank in every word, gasping in all the right places.

By the time I finished the story, I knew she wasn't going to need persuading. She was on my side. And if she was, then anyone who heard the story from her would be, too.

After she gushed about how unfair it was that I even had to go to the office, I asked her if she'd heard anything more about the new girl.

"Well, nothing except that she's *way* nice and everyone loves her. She's really popular already. It's only been like forty-eight hours since she got into town!" she said, chewing on the end of a chopstick. "Oh, my

God! You guys should totally hang out. I mentioned you on her first day, and she didn't even know who you *were* yet."

I almost asked her why she would suggest that when she knew what I'd told her about what Anna had said. Then I remembered the grenade. And then I thought about what had been happening to me.

My popularity was dwindling, and Anna's was increasing.

Inside, I felt like some kind of worst fear had been confirmed. I had to stop this Anna girl from blowing up my life. And I knew exactly how.

"Jillian?"

"Yeah?"

"How quickly can you tell everyone about the big party tomorrow night?"

"What big party?"

"The one we're going to have."

Jillian squealed and started bouncing quietly on her sofa cushion. She was obsessed with parties. Sometimes I'd wake up on the day of one of my parties, wander blearily down the stairs, and spot her outside setting up with Meredith. I was lucky to have them—I rarely had to do much.

A party was the perfect solution. It was time to

reassert my popularity. Time to show Anna who wore the skinny jeans in this town. Better too soon than too late.

"'K, so get started," I said, and Jillian nodded. I was gratified by her consistent agreeability. "Tomorrow you should get here early. We'll have to set up. Plus I've got better makeup than you do. We'll have to tell Michelle to come early also. She wears stuff from, like, the drugstore." I made a *blech* sound.

Jillian was already on her phone texting out invites.

She, Michelle and I were up until two in the morning setting up for the party. I'd inform Meredith of my plans the next day. Not that it mattered anyway, because she would be flying to Florida that afternoon.

And with that parent- and guardian-less freedom, I decided that Michelle's twenty-two-year-old brother was going to have to do something more useful than sitting around playing video games.

THE NEXT DAY, JILLIAN, Michelle and I were sitting at my kitchen table eating breakfast.

Well, mostly I was.

I was scarfing down sugary cereal. Jillian was reading the nutritional facts, eating a banana and telling me all of the reasons why I *shouldn't* be eating "that bowl of sugar." Michelle wasn't eating anything.

"Michelle, eat something." I glared at her.

"I'm not hungry, it's fine."

"Michelle."

"Seriously, Bridget."

I considered her for a moment. "What, do you not *like* what I have to eat or something?"

I narrowed my eyes at her as she exhaled edgily.

"I'm just not hungry, okay?"

My phone vibrated on the table. I silenced it, not interested in reading yet another excited text from someone I didn't care about saying something about *C ya tonite!* or *Thanks for the invite!*

We'd invited everyone we knew. And it felt like all of them were texting me. Which was all well and good—maybe people hadn't been doing what I *told* them to lately, but I seriously doubted that everyone would stop being this eager to be my friend any time soon.

"Fine," I said, as I took another bite from my cereal. "As long as you're not just overreacting to Jillian's little health freak-out over there. It's not like she even knows what she's talking about."

She didn't say anything, and just as I was about to grill her some more, Meredith came quietly into the kitchen. She was rubbing her lips together and closing a lipstick.

"Oh, good morning, girls!" She smiled.

I sneered. I didn't know why, but as soon as she walked into the room, I felt like she'd been offensive somehow.

"I'm having a party tonight," I said, giving her no greeting whatsoever.

"Are you?"

"Yes." I looked challengingly at her. Then I spotted her purse and suitcase by the front door. "I thought your flight wasn't until four. Arc you leaving *now?*"

It would be exactly like her to leave so ridiculously early for a flight. Even that conscientiousness of hers bothered me.

"Oh, well." She pulled a to-go coffee mug from the cabinet and turned around to get the milk from the fridge. "I'm meeting somebody beforehand and I'll have about an hour and a half before the shuttle picks me up after that. I just want to be ready to go in case the meeting runs long."

"Meeting with who?" I asked.

She turned back to me and looked into my eyes warily. It had something to do with me, I knew it.

*"Who?"* I demanded.

She sighed. "John Ezhno."

Of course she couldn't bring herself to lie, and save me the embarrassment she was now inflicting on me.

*"Really."* I stared at her.

"Yes, does that surprise you?"

"Um, yes." It did. I could not believe this was still going on. "Does *that* surprise *you?*"

She set down the skim milk, and looked at me.

"Bridget, stop it."

"*You* stop it." She was the one going around having secret meetings. About *me,* for God's sake.

"Bridget, I mean it! You know, I wouldn't have to keep seeing him if you or your father would just—" She stopped.

If *Meredith* started defying me, I'd start a damn war with her. I didn't have anything to lose in this relationship.

"Would just *what?*"

She dropped her head, clearly holding back more tears. Taking a deep breath, she stood up straight, secured the lid on her mug and walked out the door. I felt a small wave of guilt wash over me. I hated when other people took the high road in an argument. It made me look foolish.

When I turned back to my cereal, I felt two pairs of

eyes on me. I looked up to see Jillian's and Michelle's mouths hanging open.

"Wha…?" I said with my mouth full.

The two of them exchanged an uncomfortable look.

"Nothing," Jillian said, turning her face back to the nutritional facts. Her eyebrows were still raised.

"Look, I can't help what she's doing. You guys aren't going to tell anybody, right? Jillian?"

"Of course not. Did you know this has partially hydrogenated oils in it? That is *so* bad for you. Oh!" She stopped to answer her phone, which had just started emitting a tinny version of "Respect."

After talking for a minute, she hung up and announced that she had to go. Her brother had knocked his front tooth out, and she needed to take him to the dentist.

Michelle stuck around, which was weird, because usually she left earlier than Jillian. It was always strange when it was just the two of us. It always felt a little naked without someone else around as a buffer.

After closing the door on Jillian and reminding her to come back ASAP so I could fix her face with my makeup, I walked into the living room, where Michelle was sitting, and turned on the TV.

"Bridget?" she said. "Can we talk for a second?"

"Sure," I said, flipping through the channels. She looked at the TV, and then at me.

"Like, without the TV on?"

I exhaled noisily and turned it off. She took a deep breath before speaking.

"It's kind of…embarrassing to talk about. I just think…that you kind of…make me feel bad about myself sometimes." She said the last part of her sentence so fast I barely understood the words.

I scoffed and raised my eyebrows at her. "I what?"

"It's just…I'm sensitive about my weight and—"

She *couldn't* be serious.

"Oh, shut *up,* Michelle."

"No, Bridget, I won't shut up!" She stood up. "You say things all the time that make me feel really bad about myself, and it's just not okay!"

I sat there on the couch, looking up at her skinny body and bony cheekbones. I was shocked. I had hardly ever seen her mad about *anything,* and here she was, flipping out about something stupid.

In retrospect, I realize I should have taken her seriously, if only just because she was my friend and I owed her that.

Instead, I was embarrassed by what she'd said. I took it as an attack on me and stood up, too.

"Like *what?*"

"Oh, my God, Bridget, you really don't know?"

I suddenly felt defensive. What could I have ever said to make her feel insecure about her weight?

"No, I *really don't know,*" I said, saying her words with a nasty tone. "Are you seriously telling me *you* feel fat?"

"Yes!"

"Oh, puh-*leeze.* You're deluded. You're crazy! And I'm not going to listen to crazy talk." Not anymore, anyway. I'd had enough of that lately.

Plus, Michelle was super skinny. She was like five foot eight and a hundred and fifteen pounds. She was the kind of pretty that made you want to just eat vegetables and fruit and sacrifice all the fat/delicious in your diet. She had *always* been gorgeous. The only reason *she* wasn't the queen of the school was because she was too shy, not good with makeup or hair or clothes, and wasn't willing to claw her way to the top of the social ladder. And because I wouldn't let it happen.

But even though the situation warranted me saying something reassuring like that, I just kept shouting at her.

"*I* didn't say you're fat, Michelle. I *wouldn't* say anything like that. But if you *feel* fat, eat a salad or something, I don't know. It's all in your head. Just don't blame *your* insecurities on me!"

She was so obviously thin that this conversation seemed ridiculous, and I didn't want to waste time catering to Michelle's compliment fishing.

"It's not *my* insecurities only, Bridget, you're always making comments about what I should do to look prettier and telling me my clothes are all wrong, and I just can't—"

"I'm your friend, Michelle, it's called advice?" Then something occurred to me. I hushed my tone in disbelief at what this whole thing might be about. "Is this about the gym shorts? They're from *freshman year.* And they just don't fit you anymore!" *And there's nothing wrong with that,* I should have said.

Instead, I shushed her when she tried to talk, and turned the TV back on. We spent the next hour in awkward silence, each with our faces pointed in the direction of the TV show neither of us were interested in, pretending that the argument hadn't happened.

A FEW HOURS LATER, I wondered if what I'd said to Michelle was too harsh. I was considering dialing her number on the phone in my hand when I heard a car door slam in the driveway.

I raced down the stairs so that when Meredith opened the front door, I was standing on the bottom step with my arms crossed and my lips pursed.

She looked at me and sighed.

*She* was impatient with *me?*

"Listen, Bridget—"

"What did you guys talk about? Did you swap stories about how awful I am?"

"Bridget, please," she pleaded, quietly.

I closed my mouth only because I was desperate to hear what had happened.

She walked into the sitting room off the foyer and sat on the love seat. "Listen, I just can't talk about this right now."

My nerves twinged. I had to know what happened. They were talking about *my life.* "You can't just go off with *my* teacher and then refuse to tell me what happened, Meredith."

"I'm not *refusing.*" Her voice was weary. "I just have other things on my mind, and—"

"If you would just say it, this conversation would end so much sooner."

She shut her eyes, and took a deep breath.

It started to seem like it really wasn't the right time, and I was just about to tell her to forget it and just tell me later, but then she started talking.

"He's fed up with you being disrespectful. You and he, he and I, you and I, have *all* had that conversation. It is just time you stop. You don't want to be removed from the class and have to take it again."

"Obviously. Did he say that he might kick me out of class?"

"He just mentioned it as being an option. Honestly, we only spoke for a few minutes."

I squinted my eyes.

"But you were gone for, like, three hours."

"Yes, Bridget, I was doing other things as well."

*My life doesn't revolve around you* was her implication.

And—strangely, ridiculously—that hurt my feelings.

"*What* were you doing?" I wanted to know.

"Enough!" she shouted, with a burst of energy I had not seen coming.

It felt like a slap in the face. I stared at her, unable to speak.

She stood up. "Why are you like this, Bridget?"

"Why am I like *what?*" I took a step back, feeling suddenly like I couldn't predict what Meredith might do. I wouldn't have guessed she would ever shout at me.

My *real* mother wouldn't have shouted at me. Surely.

"So rude all the time! It doesn't matter if I try to help you, or if I try to do something nice, it's never *enough!* I've been in your life for the last seven years, and you *still* treat me like the evil stepmother. Last I remember, the biggest request I made of you was to let *me* take you to a movie you wanted to see! And yet you sit here with your friends, and put me on the spot..."

She stopped talking, her eyes scanning the ground, like she was looking for a way to express herself.

I defended myself against the indefensible. "I don't even know what you're talking about—"

"I tried to leave the house this morning by simply saying I was off to meet someone. I didn't *want* to mention that I was going to have a meeting with Mr. Ezhno, because I was trying not to embarrass you!"

"Why should *I* be embarrassed? You two are the ones who keep meeting to—"

"Because, Bridget!" She ran her manicured fingers through the big curls in her blond hair. "You're too old for this. I can't believe your teachers are *still* calling parent-teacher meetings, just like they were when you were in sixth grade. Usually, at this age, you would have earned independence and trust from your family, by acting like an adult—or no, not even an adult. Just simply by acting your age, instead of trying to get attention by being the class clown and terrorizing your teachers and everyone else you go to school with."

I gaped at her, my chest heaving, my face hot, not knowing what to say. I had never heard Meredith raise her voice. I'd never seen her angry. I'd certainly never expected her to be so angry with *me.* That wasn't how *we* worked.

In our relationship, *she* tried to please *me,* and *I* made the decisions.

It had always been that way.

Why was she turning on me now? Why, when I was already so stressed out, was she suddenly playing evil stepmother?

"Well, maybe," I said calmly, pulling out my metaphorical bazooka, "I was never taught manners. I mean, the only *real* mother I had died in a car accident before you came to live here. *She* was the only one who ever *really* loved us, but she's gone and you've just taken over."

Meredith was silent. She opened her mouth to say

something but apparently changed her mind and closed it again.

The intimidation I'd felt briefly was gone. I took a step toward her. "So obviously, if you're going to be all parental, I'm not the right one to do it with. And let's face it, it's not your thing."

Meredith winced, put a hand on her stomach, and sat back down on the love seat.

Now *that* was a bit dramatic.

Still…I could see that I had hurt her feelings. It wasn't like I'd wanted to do that. Or at least I hadn't wanted to do that without first feeling provoked. But there was nothing I could really do about it now. However upset she was, I was probably the last person she wanted consoling from, even if it had been me who had upset her.

And then, as I did every time I felt guilty (don't ask me why), I pretended I didn't care at all. I scoffed, and walked up the stairs as casually as possible, not looking behind me. I was glad the airport shuttle would be taking her away any minute now.

When I got into my room, I sat on the edge of my bed and wondered what to do next.

What was *with* everyone?

I knew I wasn't the one who had changed. It was like everyone else had gone crazy.

It was like an episode of *The Twilight Zone.*

Even Michelle was acting weird. The only other time I'd ever seen her that mad was in sixth grade. And that time, at least, I'd understood why she was mad.

I'd had a different set of friends at the time. Bratty, loud, obnoxious, bullying girls. I started hanging around with them after my mom's accident. I actually remember deciding that if I couldn't have a mother, then at the very least I was going to have friends. I chose them because they had the power. Honestly, a psychologist would have had a field day with me, I was so transparent.

At the time, I was not at all popular. And even *I* could see that the girls I hung around with were bad influences. They pulled pranks, teased the other girls, were nasty to teachers and did anything else they could think of to have control over their peers. It wasn't like I even liked them. Liam, a good friend to me even then, always told me I could do better.

But they were the ones everyone listened to, so that was who I acquainted myself with. I spent the entire "friendship" running behind them, telling them that I didn't think whatever they were planning was a very good idea. That's probably why they let me hang around with them for those four years—so that they could feel impressive and outrageous without necessarily getting caught.

But the one trick I did get blamed for entirely was the one they pulled on Michelle. As I said, it happened in sixth grade, during Outdoor Ed.

Outdoor Ed. To me, this seemed like the bad idea of some hippie who thought it wise to send a bunch of eleven- and twelve-year-olds to crawl around in the woods, barely supervised.

The Event with Michelle happened on the second night in the cabins.

I had just seen *The Parent Trap* at the time, and I was eager to come up with something similar to—but less messy than—the honey and toilet paper scene from the movie. I was eager to come up with a good prank instead of always being the follower. They had decided that Michelle was the perfect target, as she was generally considered to be the prettiest girl in school.

Michelle had always been nice to me. Foolishly, rather than figuring that she might be a bad person to prank, I figured she might forgive me. So I agreed to do it to her.

My friends and I snuck off from the nightly campfire

and tiptoed back to the cabin that we, Michelle and three other girls were staying in, stifling giggles the whole way.

One of the girls I was friends with, Melissa, had come up with the idea of squirting shampoo and some other substances into the sheets and under the blanket, so Michelle wouldn't know until she crawled under the sheets. We all had to take showers across the property, and she wouldn't get an opportunity to wash up until the next day.

The other two girls were all for it. I, being the moral (my word, not theirs) one of the group, thought that it wouldn't be fair to make the bed impossible to sleep in, to incapacitate her in that way. That would be cruel.

When I said that, they just stared at me.

So I said that we would *probably* get caught if we were the ones with the shampoo that smelled the same. I also pointed out that if and when she was forced to tattle on us, we'd have to all stay awake and in trouble until they got new sheets for her and that the chaperones probably *would* walk her over to the showers.

Jenny, the leader of the group, shrugged and told me to come up with something better. I scrambled to come up with something tame, but still cool enough to satisfy them.

I was still thinking when Tammy, the girl whose name I longed for at the time, shrieked.

I gasped when I looked up to see her pulling something out of Michelle's Cinderella bag, which everyone had made fun of her for bringing. We all said it was babyish. The truth was that I loved it, and hated her for having not only the bag, but also the confidence to bring it with her, despite the risk of being mocked.

Tammy pulled out a lump of tin foil and ran over to us to show us what she'd found inside.

Kotex. Sanitary pads.

I remember feeling shocked. Shocked that Tammy had dug through someone else's things (although a moment later I remembered that it was Tammy we were talking about, and that it was par for her course); shocked that a girl in our grade already had her period; and then shocked that *we* were the ones to find out. I shuddered to think what trick they were going to pull with this knowledge.

As soon as Melissa and Jenny saw the pads, they instantly jumped into action. Jenny told Melissa to go get the red nail polish she'd snuck into the cabins and asked Tammy if she had any more Butterfinger candy bars with her. Jenny herself started laying the pads out on the ground, for reasons I couldn't have imagined.

I watched in private horror as they dripped nail polish and water onto the pads and smeared chocolate onto one side. I couldn't do anything to stop them. If I said anything, I knew they would just do something like this—or possibly far worse—to me as retribution.

Rumor had it that Jenny had actually punched people before.

They peeled the backs off the pads and started sticking them to the frame of the bunk bed Michelle was sleeping in.

When they finally finished, they stuffed away the evidence and stood back to look at their work.

"Nice, ladies," Jenny said, her hands on her hips. Tammy and Melissa laughed.

"There's only five minutes left 'til the end of campfire. We'd better go," I said, suddenly feeling like there was no time at all. I had to get out of there, away from all of that mess and meanness and impending humiliation.

They agreed and headed out. I said I had to pee and would be right behind them.

None of them responded, and they continued walking.

As soon as they were gone, I started pulling down the pads. I was just pulling down the third one when I heard the cabin door open. I stood there, frozen, with nowhere to go or hide.

Melissa, Jenny and Tammy were back and standing there, mouths agape. And then they started to laugh loudly and enthusiastically.

A second later, our other roommates came in. After what felt like another mere second, there were even more. And they were all laughing. I couldn't tell if it was at me or at what they thought I was doing. Maybe it was at Michelle. I just couldn't tell. The survival instinct in me just wanted them to direct it at someone else.

With a start, I saw what they saw.

*I* looked like the perpetrator.

And then, finally, Michelle came into the room.

Before Michelle could react, the parent chaperone—Mr. Lambert—walked in. Seeming to understand immediately what was happening, he shouted my name and told me to come with him. Still frozen, I stood still, watching more and more faces come into the room. It seemed like every girl in camp piled in to see what I had done, and even some of the boys stuck their heads in to have a good guffaw.

When I finally was able to move my eyes to Michelle, I saw that she was standing just as frozen as I was, staring at me. Looking livid.

I gave her a pleading look.

What happened next passed by in such a flurry that I hardly knew what happened. I was vaguely aware of Mr. Lambert taking me by my upper arm, talking on his official-looking walkie-talkie, Michelle shouting at me, and the faces of Melissa, Jenny and Tammy turning red from all the suppressed—and unsuppressed—laughing.

The rest of the night passed in much the same way. I was in an office, I was being reprimanded, I had to call and tell Meredith—then my new stepmother—what I'd done, and I had to go back to the shameful limelight of the cabin to pack my things. Escorted, and then supervised.

The next thing I knew, I was in Meredith's Land Rover, on the way home.

We were silent during the ride, until I felt my throat tighten and my eyes start to sting. I started crying and couldn't stop. Meredith told me to calm down and that she wouldn't tell my father, who was out of town for a game at the time.

When we got home, she made me a mug of warm vanilla milk—a tradition she told me was from her childhood (but that I was unfamiliar with). It soothed me enough that I finally fell asleep with my head in Meredith's lap, with her stroking my hair.

When I woke up the next morning, it was to the sound of the phone ringing. I answered, groggily, and heard the voice of my father on the other end.

"Bridget Jane Duke! What is *wrong* with you? How could you *do* that to Michelle?"

He continued on like that, not stopping once to hear my explanation, completely typical for him. I said nothing, thinking only about the fact that Meredith had sworn she wouldn't tell anyone. I'd think about that for the rest of the school year, which I spent grounded.

*I* knew *I shouldn't like her,* I thought to myself scathingly. She'd seen my parents' big house, my father's limited fame and fortune and that my mother was out of the picture. And she'd glommed on.

From then on, I hated her.

## CHAPTER FOUR

"I guess we'll do...fifteen large pizzas...make five regular cheese, five pepperoni and the rest of them...I don't know, Hawaiian or something. Okay, is it cool if I pay now over the phone, and you deliver them at ten-thirty? Awesome, okay, so the credit card number is..." I scrambled around the kitchen looking for the "for emergencies only, please" note and credit card Meredith had left me, making "um" noises as I searched. When I finally found it, I read the number and expiration date to the pothead-sounding pizza guy on the other end of the phone.

"And the name on the card?" he asked, sounding bored.

"Meredith Duke. Do you need me to spell it?"

"Nope. Got it."

No, I didn't ask to use it for pizzas, but I figured it would be fine; it's what Meredith always did for my parties. When she wasn't mad at me.

Plus, saving my popularity was a total emergency.

I was confirming the order when I heard the doorbell ring.

"'K, so then I'm all set, right? I have to go, thanks, 'bye." I hung up the phone and ran.

I opened the door to a hauntingly familiar sight that I hadn't seen in over a year.

Liam, on my doorstep, hair mussed the way it always was, clothes casual but perfect, skin perpetually tanned from actual sun instead of the fake bake I used. The only difference was that he wasn't smiling at me like he always used to. And that was a big difference.

It wasn't until he spoke that I realized I'd been staring at him with my mouth open.

"Got a sec?" he asked, in a tone I didn't quite recognize.

"Uh, yeah, I guess, I'm just setting up for the party." Then I remembered the cooler in the garage. "Actually, if you could help me move something—"

"Sure, but let's talk first."

He stepped into the house, and in the split second

when he stood next to me and *didn't* look at me, I started feeling panicky. It was disconcerting how accustomed I was to seeing him in my house, and at the same time how completely out of place he seemed. It was like seeing the president in his old elementary school classroom.

Except that *I* was the reason Liam hadn't been back.

The reason he didn't *want* to come back.

I was so distracted by how intimidating he seemed that I forgot to wonder why he was there, wanting to talk to me.

I followed him into my living room. When he sat, I sat.

"What's up, Liam?" I always felt like a suck-up when I talked to him nowadays, despite my efforts to seem casual.

He still wasn't looking at me. "The party, Bridget. I just want to make sure you're not planning any kind of embarrassment for Anna."

Instantly all the unresolved feelings from our breakup congealed in the pit of my stomach.

"*Anna?* The new girl?" As if I didn't know. "I'd never—"

"Yes, you would." His tone challenged me to object.

I knew if I did, he'd walk.

Instead, I asked, "What's with you two, anyway?"

"Does that mean you *were* planning something if she showed up here?"

"Oh, come on, Liam, I'm not the wicked witch. I can be civilized, you know." I thought of the drink-spilling trick I *wasn't* planning for Anna's shirt later on. The trick that involved me giving her a shirt of mine to wear, and it being too small and therefore unflattering on her.

(And me, but I wouldn't tell her that.)

"Listen," Liam said, "I'm just saying that I don't think you should do anything. I know you're probably pissed about her being so well-liked already and stuff, but don't take it out on her." He sounded like a grown-up talking about high school drama. Maybe that should have told me something, but it didn't.

"I don't understand why you're so worried about it."

He hung his head, and answered into his hands. "Because she's a nice girl, and I know you."

*...are not* was what he was saying.

That wasn't true.

It *wasn't.*

"You don't know me. Not anymore." I felt the petty *I'm-still-not-over-it* words come out of my mouth, and any of the cool I did have left me.

"Whatever, I know the social homicide you're capable of committing. Just don't do it."

I clenched my jaw. I hated when he talked to me like a child.

"I won't," I said, and he finally looked me in the eyes. I smiled, and held up my hand like a Boy Scout. "Bitch's honor."

Some part of me hated that I had to play that role even with him.

He looked at me for a moment, and I felt the chill in my chest soften my expression. Just for that moment, we were *us.* The old us, where I was just goofy and outrageous and he was indulgent. Where we were real with each other. Sometimes I missed that. Sometimes I wanted to just throw down the crown I wore at school and be his again.

But that would be foolish. He wouldn't take me back anyway.

I was shaken from my reverie when he cleared his throat and asked, "All right, what do you need me to move?"

"Cooler."

"What did you do, load it before putting it outside?"

I nodded sheepishly. He shook his head with a smile, and muttered my name. "Ah, Bridget. Where is it?"

"Garage."

He immediately turned and headed toward the garage. The garage with the side door I used to sneak him in through when we were younger. A moment later, he came through the kitchen with the cooler, the veins on his forearms raised.

"Deck?"

I nodded again and flitted to the sliding door to open it for him. I leaned on the doorframe and watched him put the cooler down. After setting it neatly against the fence of the deck, he walked toward me, stopping in front of me.

"Anything else?"

I felt a little winded as I hurried to try and think of something else I needed him to do.

I couldn't. "I don't think so." When he kept looking at me, I added, "But thanks."

"All right then, I guess I'll see you later."

My heart skipped a clichéd beat.

"Literally, later? Like, you're coming to the party?"

Wow, did that sound desperate. But I had to make

sure. He rarely came to my parties, and it was often only when I asked him to personally.

He gave a single laugh, "Yeah, literally."

"'K, then." He was coming. He thought Anna was coming. Was that because he was *bringing* her? Or because he just assumed she'd heard about it like everyone else? I decided it had to be the latter. "Oh! Bring your bathing suit!"

"Aw, no, Bridge, does that mean *you're* going to be swimming? Are you going to do any 'awesome new tricks' you learned?" He laughed a real laugh, and I knew he was remembering the embarrassing episode I'd had at the pool when we were eleven. And the front-toothless school picture that had followed. It still hung in the front hall.

I narrowed my eyes at him and smiled playfully. "At least I didn't pee in the pool, *Wee-um*."

"I was like five," he said coolly, and opened the front door, "and I was trapped in the deep end."

"Ha." I felt my uncreative response end the moment.

Liam gave a short laugh and started down the front steps.

"Okay, see you later," he said again, then added, "literally."

He pulled on the key lanyard that hung from his front pocket and got into his black SUV.

I watched him go and not look back.

Then I turned back to the house and went in. I closed the door and walked absentmindedly into the kitchen to make a sandwich so I wouldn't be so hungry that I'd pig out on pizza at the party.

It was always weird seeing Liam. Probably weirder for me than for him, I guessed. Though maybe it shouldn't have been. I mean, we'd known each other forever.

We'd met in elementary school, and as kids he'd been my number-one advocate, no matter what the situation. When I was bullied, he was there standing up for me. When my mom died, he was there comforting me—which isn't an easy feat for a child.

When we were younger we'd spent every recess, every lunch period and every bus ride together. Once we were a little older and had a little more independence, we walked to and from school together and still went to lunch together. He was the best part of my day for a really long time. And he stuck by me, even when I was stupid enough to be friends with the girls who planned the Outdoor Ed event.

It was in high school that our relationship changed.

We'd been repainting my room—which I insisted

upon doing myself, and not with the help of Todd the Professional—when a moment came upon us. I don't know where it came from, or who initiated it. All I know is that one second we were squirting each other with a spray bottle of Rust-Oleum, and the next we were kissing.

For the rest of the summer, we'd been entirely blissful together. I didn't see the girls I'd been hanging around with (it was mostly an in-school friendship), and I felt more like myself than I had since I was a kid.

He thought I was fun and wild (I knew because I asked him why he liked me every two and a half seconds), and I thought he was super cute, strong, funny, sweet…

We spent the days at the pool or walking his dog (I didn't have one of my own, thanks to Meredith's stupid allergy), and the nights on the phone or watching movies. In the wee hours of the morning, when we would sometimes still be on the phone, we would sneak out and meet each other in the field between our houses. We'd lie on the thin-bladed grass and stare up at the sky, watching as the sunrise turned from orange to purple to blue, and talk about everything we could think of.

How we were still able to come up with new topics for that long, I have no idea.

Now it felt like we had nothing to say at all.

I left my just-made and uneaten sandwich on the counter and set off to lose myself in party decorating.

By seven o'clock, I had worked diligently to get the party set up. It was important to me that this party be perfect, that it help to reassert my reputation.

The streamers were hung and laced through the lattices, the strings of twinkling white Christmas lights were twisted around the tree branches, the food was set up and covered, the cooler was filled and a big bucket of ice was waiting to be filled with beer.

This party had to be amazing. Had to be big. People had to have fun. And the only way to ensure that everyone had fun was to have alcohol. Lots of it. It just worked out perfectly that Meredith and my dad weren't home and that we didn't have to be sneaky about that part.

I had given Michelle one of the two credit cards Meredith had left behind for emergencies and told her to convince her brother to get a bunch of beer for the party, and reminded her to get it at the grocery store. Meredith would quickly figure out what I'd used the card for if Beers & Cheers showed up on her transaction summary.

I was standing in my closet, looking hopelessly at the limp abominations on the hangers, when the doorbell rang.

"Come in!" I shouted. I heard the front door open and then two pairs of footsteps coming up the stairs.

"Hey, Bridget!" Jillian said, plunking herself down on my cushy bed.

"Hey," I replied, and then looked at Michelle, who was holding a six-pack of Corona in each hand, "Do you need help bringing in the rest of the beer? Jillian, why don't you help her?"

I was, after all, busy. I turned back to my closet. There was a moment of silence before I heard Michelle's quiet voice.

"The *rest* of the beer?"

I froze, the creeping, hesitant feeling of realization washing over me. I turned to Jillian. "Tell me there's a 'rest of the beer.'"

Her already wide eyes widened more as she pulled her eyebrows into a desperate, worried expression. I looked at Michelle. She was biting her lip, and had the same expression on her face as Jillian.

I gave a humorless laugh, before shaking my head.

"What the hell is *wrong* with you, Michelle? God, it's like you're stupid or something. One minute you're telling me you're all insecure about *everything* and the next minute you're ruining my party." I looked into her eyes. "Great job. Seriously."

"But Bridget, you just said to get some beer, you didn't say how much you—"

"I gave you Meredith's credit card and told you to get beer for the party, how is it *not* obvious that you're going to need more?" I spoke quietly, but I was livid. And I was worried, too. I had been depending on the alcohol to make the party a success. Depending on it to give me the confidence to try and get Liam back. "And if you had *any* question about it, why didn't you just call and *ask?*"

"I tried! You didn't pick up!"

"Liar," I said, and then remembered my phone lying on the floor of the garage where I'd left it when I was filling the cooler with soda. I hadn't seen it in hours.

"I'm sorry, it was stupid—" Michelle started.

"You're right, so why are you still here?"

She looked up at me, looking a little panicked.

"What do you mean?"

"I *mean* why aren't you driving back to get your brother to go buy more?"

I saw a glimmer of relief on her face, before a new fear seemed to take hold.

"Um. Well, he's not at home."

I laughed again, "I'm sorry, *what?* Your brother has been sitting in that stupid gaming chair since we were like, six, what do you mean he's not home?"

"He went out with a friend—"

I didn't let her finish. "*God,* Michelle. Now what the hell are we going to do?"

Jillian piped up. "I might…have an idea."

"What?" I asked, crossing my arms. I was *not* optimistic about anything Jillian might come up with.

"What about your dad's bar?"

"I can't use that stuff, he'll kill me."

"Are you sure he'll notice?" Jillian asked.

"Am I sure he'll *notice?* Yes, I'm sure he'll—" I had an idea. "Ooh, but you know who won't notice? *Your* dad. He drinks like, all the time, he'll just think he drank it and buy more."

I saw that she regretted the idea now that it was being turned on her. "I don't know, Bridge."

"Oh, stop it, we both know you're going to do it, so just go so you can come back. Just fill the rest of the bottles back up with water when the party's over. To him it will probably taste just the same. I'll try and take a little of my dad's, too." Jillian didn't move. "Go!"

She stood up and pushed her way past Michelle. By the time I heard her car start, I was already back in my closet looking for something decent to wear. I was barely aware that Michelle was still there.

"Bridget, I…"

No way. There was no way we were going to do this now. "It's probably not a good idea to talk to me right now. If I were you, I'd just go do something about your makeup." I locked my eyes on her outfit. "And you'll probably want to change."

She looked for a moment like she was going to say something, but then turned around and headed for the bathroom, where my makeup was.

"Don't use my mascara, it's not sanitary to share it."

She'd shared it a million times, but I was mad. She was not going to waste my good mascara after how dumb she'd acted.

After about thirty outfit changes, on the part of both Michelle and myself, Jillian's car came squealing back into the driveway. The next thing I knew she was panting in my doorframe. I peered at her from the bathroom, where I was moisturizing my face.

"What?" I glared at the eyeliner that was beneath her eyes and in need of tidying. We were never going to be ready for this party.

"I…got…." She tried to catch her breath. "Pulled…over."

I felt a twinge in my stomach, and my fingers froze on my cheeks, where I was applying my Hourglass cream bronzer.

"Did you have the stuff in your car?" I needed to know.

She nodded, and my stomach lurched again.

"Do you *still?*"

She nodded again.

"Well, then no harm, no foul." Not that she hadn't freaked me out but I didn't need to *stay* freaked, the way she apparently planned to.

I started rubbing in the bronzer again.

"Bridget!" Jillian shouted, and I looked back at her.

"What?" I made a point to emphasize the *t.* Man, was I tired of people having freak-outs.

"Bridget, omigod, I could have gotten *arrested.* Don't you even care?"

"But you weren't, so…"

"So, nothing, Bridget, I almost got caught with like

twelve bottles of liquor and a thirty-pack of Natty Light in my back seat!"

"Twelve bottles and a thirty?"

"Yes!" she said, insistently.

"That's great, good job." I wiped my hands on the towel that hung on a ring next to the sink.

"That's not the point! I got pulled over for a taillight being out, and I almost got arrested for underage possession of alcohol! And I don't even *drink!*"

I sighed. Why wasn't she sharing this story as a victory, instead of worrying about something that was already over and that, more to the point, *didn't* happen?

"Okay, Jillian, you have *got* to calm down. First of all, you didn't get caught, so stop flipping out. Second of all, you do not need to be such a buzz kill. What you *do* need to do is to bring in the bottles, put them outside on the table and cheer up. Because you're really annoying me right now. You *and* Michelle."

At that moment, Michelle came into the room. She'd been going through Meredith's clothes, upon my instruction and insistence that it was fine for her to do so. I didn't want her to look better in something of mine. She was wearing a form-fitting black dress that looked awesome on her.

"What about this?" she asked, smiling.

"Too tight." I said after a half a glance in her direction. It wasn't really, but I didn't need her looking better in something of Meredith's either. Normally, I wouldn't be that way, but it was a big deal for me to look good to Liam. It was like a bride on her wedding day—it's just unfair for a bridesmaid to look better. Except this wasn't a wedding, it was a bash where I was going to try to look good enough that Liam would forget about why we broke up.

Michelle left the room again. Jillian was still watching me.

"Bridget, it could have been like a huge deal."

"Well, it's not! God, Jillian, chill!"

She squinted her eyes at me. Irritated. "Fine. But I'm never doing that again."

I was more irritated by far. "Don't worry, you won't need to do anything for my next party. You don't even really have to show up." Not if she was going to act like that.

I knew that the truth was that I would probably have reacted the same way. I also knew that I could have just as easily gotten the wrong amount of beer. I knew that I was lucky to even have friends to help me with the party. I was lucky that they would get alcohol even when they weren't necessarily interested in having any themselves.

But I couldn't say any of that. Couldn't *worry* about any of that when I had the party to think of. I figured they'd either forgive me privately or decide they *had* been stupid and apologize.

It was what always happened.

And with that thought, I finished putting on my makeup, told Michelle how good she looked in a high necked, conservative dress, and told Jillian to go to the store and pick up the cookies I'd forgotten to buy.

## CHAPTER FIVE

"Right foot red!" Martin, the linebacker for the school football team, shouted, popping open the top of a Corona he'd just been handed.

I stretched my foot to the nearest red dot. My last remaining competitor in our game of Twister was a gawky girl named Sandy. A couple of guys I barely knew had brought it with them, and on a dare, I was playing the game and had promised to get other girls to do the same.

I acted grudging about doing it, rolling my eyes, saying how I'd do it only because they dared me. Frankly, though, I would jump at nearly any chance to show off my flexibility and ability to do a perfect backbend. Never was there a game with such opportunity to appear innocent and not at the same time.

My eagerness was only heightened by the fact that Liam was outside, too. Sure, he was playing football with a couple of other guys, but I was sure he could toss a few glances my way.

I landed my foot effortlessly on the red dot by snaking my leg through my opponent's knees, a tactic that got a lot of encouraging "oohs" and whistles from my audience—which was mostly guys. I looked up at the crowd and smiled.

Sandy slid her foot toward the red dot, and then slipped. In our slightly altered state, it seemed like the funniest thing that had ever happened. I was laughing so hard I barely noticed when Martin placed the cardboard crown—stolen from the kids' meal at a cheap restaurant someone had been to that evening—on my head.

I looked up to see Liam smiling at me from across the yard. In an entirely characteristic move, he shook his head and laughed.

He used to do it all the time with me, as if to say, "Oh, Bridget, you're really something."

I smiled back and, with a huge effort to be the first of us, looked away. I hoped that he watched me go, thinking wistfully of how he missed my crazy antics. But I suspected he'd probably just gone back to his game, and that if I could read his thoughts I would be disappointed by how me-less they were.

The next hour of the party carried on exactly as I'd hoped. Everyone was up, talking, playing games and laughing. No one was sitting around exchanging looks about how bored they were and trying just to stay as long as was polite—which had always been my biggest fear as a child, and the reason I never had birthday parties.

It wasn't until I started hanging around with Jenny's crowd that I finally felt like people would stay at a party I had. Even if it was just because they were afraid Tammy would pull their hair out if they didn't.

I floated around the party, paying attention to a few people at a time, and each time being pulled away and having to give a secretly self-impressed "Sorry, I have to go!" before carrying on with the new activity. It felt like my life was getting back to normal.

If I said something, people listened.

If I had a plan, people were excited to participate.

If I took off my clothes and dove into the pool wearing a black bikini, people—well, *guys*—watched and eventually jumped in, too.

I even sort of enjoyed the nasty looks from the other girls who were wearing makeup that would wipe right off and hadn't thought to bring a bathing suit—it meant they were jealous.

It meant I was back to being *me.*

At around ten-fifteen, the doorbell rang, and, assuming it was the pizza guy, I shouted "Pizza!" and everyone cheered. I find that at a party it is easy to get everyone excited about everything. I could have shouted "Dishwasher detergent!" and everyone would have been just as excited.

I ran toward the door, still wearing my bikini and only a sheer sarong around my hips. The cardboard crown had been perched upon my head again, and as I figured, aptly.

I opened the door to see Anna.

My gut lurched as I reasserted my mental direction from flirting for a discount to appearing entirely nonchalant.

"Oh," I said, the disappointment ringing in my tone, "we all thought you were the pizza guy."

Anna smiled and raised an eyebrow at my implication that everyone was as disappointed as I was. It was a tactic I used in arguments, too—implying that "everybody says so."

"Sorry, then. I'm not the pizza guy exactly…but I did bring the pizzas."

"What does that mean?"

"It means you called and placed your order with my friend. Since I was coming here anyway, I said I'd bring it."

*What?*

"Um." Had she trumped me? I wasn't sure. "Okay, well…whatever then…I guess—"

"And I picked up the check for it, too." She was still smiling as she watched my face for reaction. "Since you're throwing the party, I figured I'd contribute something."

My jaw tightened, and I felt a wave of fury wash over me. Who did she think she was? Was this supposed to be charity? I was about to give her a piece of my mind when she stepped inside, past me.

"Everyone!" She waited a moment for the hum to quiet, and weirdly, it did. "There's a bunch of pizzas in my back seat—can anyone help me bring them in?"

A bunch of guys hurried toward her, giving her high fives on the way to the car, telling her how awesome it was of her to bring pizza for everyone. I'd never heard half of these people be polite, and here they were thanking Anna for something they should have been thanking *me* for.

Or Meredith.

Whatever.

They walked right by me, suddenly paying me no attention. I stood motionless, feeling like a car on the side of a highway being shaken by the wind from every other passing vehicle, none of them stopping to help.

I decided the only thing I could do was to keep moving and ignore what Anna had just done. The only way I could be cooler than she was would be to not show that she'd bothered me.

I walked up to her, and put an arm around her shoulders.

"That was very nice of you to do for everyone here at the party." Because she most *certainly* would not get away with saying she did it just for me.

"No problem, Bridget. It was really my pleasure," she replied, without a trace of superficiality, and then walked away.

I needed another drink. But first I needed to check my makeup and be sure I still looked my best, particularly now that *she* was here. I ran upstairs, away from the party. The echoing of my kitten heels on the wooden steps brought back a vague memory of a party of my mother's when I was very young.

I'd been set up in my parents' room with popcorn and *Cinderella,* and was told that downstairs was a grown-up party and that I was to stay where I was unless there was an emergency. After a few hours, the movie was over and I was still awake. I had put the movie back on from the beginning, and started to raid my mother's closet. I'd found a turquoise slip and a mismatched pair of high heels.

Then, after finding a Redskins hat—which I thought would be the perfect piece to complete the outfit—on my father's side of the closet, I'd headed downstairs as proud as could be. A few minutes later, I'd been sent back up with another movie and a lot of praise for being so cute. I can hardly remember ever being so content.

I was a lot more proud of myself back then.

I reached the top of the stairs and headed toward my bathroom. I was still feeling melancholy when I opened the door to see Michelle vomiting into the toilet.

We both shrieked, and I closed the door partway again.

"What the hell?" I said, my memories of size-six

heels on size-three feet replaced by the puzzle of Michelle having a reaction that could, at a moment like this, only come from overdoing the alcohol. "Michelle, what's going on? You don't drink!"

I stood on the other side of the door, utterly confused.

"I know that, Bridget!" Michelle's gasp echoed around the porcelain of the bathroom.

This was just too weird. I couldn't find any tact. "Is that the problem? Wait, I didn't even see you with a drink, how did you drink enough in two hours to get sick? What is going *on?*" No answer. "Michelle?" I heard the toilet flush, and opened the door again to stick my head in the bathroom.

She was sitting against the wall on the floor, one of her flip-flops a few inches from her bare foot. She was sobbing into her hands, which were white and wet. Her face was purple. Something wasn't right.

"Michelle, what the hell is going on here?" I grabbed a washcloth, dampened it and then bent down to press it to her forehead.

"Nothing. You wouldn't get it anyway."

"What?"

"I have the flu, I think. I don't know."

Oh, god. All I needed was for everyone to get

the flu and talk about how it had started at Bridget's Puke Party.

"Well." I thought my words out carefully, trying not to seem insensitive. "You aren't, like, staying here, then? You want to go home?"

She looked up at me, mascara running down her cheeks.

"I mean, not because of anything except, you know, the flu thing. You don't want to get everyone else sick. And you probably need to get some sleep." I scrambled to make what I was saying not sound bad. I pressed the washcloth to each of her cheeks, wiping away the mascara.

I just didn't want drama or disease or anything at this party. Was that so much to ask? I wanted it to go smoothly.

"Yeah..." she agreed vaguely.

Remembering why I came upstairs, I stood and checked my face in the mirror. I looked drunk. Which I wasn't, really, the makeup had just faded into my skin from the water and everything. Nevertheless, I did not look my best.

My eyes were less open than I'd thought they'd been, and my skin was pale. My dependable mascara kept me looking good, but I was in dire need of lipgloss and blush. I was about to apply the gloss when I remembered Michelle doing her makeup with my stuff earlier.

"You didn't…use this, right?" I held up the lip-gloss.

"No." She stood up.

"'K. Normally, you know, you can use my stuff. But I mean…" I let it hang. It would be rude to say that it was because of her nasty flu spit. Which, I mean, it was.

"I'm just gonna go, I guess. So I'll talk to you later."

"Sure." I looked at the dress she was wearing. "Do you want me to wash that or do you think you'll just do it? I'll just tell Meredith you needed to borrow it, no big deal." I tried to sound reassuring, but it came off as brash and uncaring.

"I'll do it," she said quietly as she opened the door to leave. "Jillian left already, by the way. Did you notice? Her parents called and made her come home."

Only then did I realize I hadn't seen Jillian all night.

"Feel better!" I shouted after the door closed behind her.

A few minutes later I was back downstairs. My hair

was re-poofed and I had more color in my face than most of the other girls who'd had too much to drink and didn't have their full makeup kits with them.

I'd also spent most of the night putting a bottle to my mouth and taking a small sip, holding back most of the liquid with my lips. The surrounding people always cheered and said things like "This girl can drink!" or something else about how I could really hold my liquor, and other impressed things.

As I walked down the stairs, I heard something that made the sound of Michelle's vomiting practically melodious.

The chanting of Anna's name.

I gritted my teeth. I'd spent the whole night trying to be impressive to everyone with how much I could drink (or pretend to drink), and now she was down there getting her *name chanted?* The best I got was picked up and spun around. Which only made me dizzy.

I walked outside to see Anna, who was not out-drinking me. Instead, she was doing a handstand.

"What is she doing?" I asked Lucy, a cheerleader, who was standing near me. "And why?"

"She just did two cartwheels, a back handspring, and has been holding this handstand for like a minute.

Some of the guys are placing bets on how long she can keep it up!"

"Huh," I said, trying to sound unimpressed.

"We're thinking of asking her to be on the squad," said Tina, the smallest of the cheerleaders.

"Really?" I responded, unable to keep the note of desperation from my voice. I'd always wanted to be a cheerleader. When I was a kid, I'd been on a squad that accepted anyone who paid. I'd been so uncoordinated that they gave the money back to my father so that I'd be off the team. Ever since then, I'd said that it was a childhood ankle injury that kept me from accepting a position on the team.

I watched as Anna curved her feet behind her head and landed gracefully on the grass, stretched into a backbend. I knew she looked better than I had when I'd been playing Twister. She stood up from there and curtsied. Everyone cheered.

This made no sense whatsoever. I happened to *know* that it took more than just *that* kind of thing to impress these people.

It felt like they were all doing it specifically to mortify me. Like they knew about my childhood dream and my jealousy of Anna's instant popularity, and they were doing everything in their power to make the situation harder for me. But I guessed I was the last thought on anyone's mind.

I grabbed the bottle of tequila from the table next to me and put it to my lips. And this time, I really drank. Three huge gulps. My face contorted into something that surely resembled the Warheads candy logo, and my tongue burned.

I knew how tired it was to drink because of emotions, but this wasn't just about that. I needed to be confident. Besides, it was my party and I could drink if I wanted to.

Unfortunately, the rest of the party just felt like the Anna Judge Show. Everyone seemed hypnotized by her, and no one was paying any attention to me. I even came up with the idea of skinny-dipping, and no one was interested.

Isn't *everyone* supposed to be interested in that kind of thing in high school?

Eventually my attention—and only my attention—shifted from Anna to myself.

The last double shot of tequila, which I'd immediately regretted having, had turned my stomach into Jell-O. Apparently I was learning the hard way that alcohol doesn't solve problems. Instead, it made everything that much harder. But it wasn't until I found myself alone with Liam that I realized how difficult it was to be charming when you kind of wanted to puke.

By that point almost everyone had fallen asleep or gotten a ride home, and the people who were left were watching a movie Anna had brought with her. A movie that hadn't been released yet—she'd gotten it straight from the production company. I had left the room before finding out how.

I had just been about to nod off myself when I discovered that one of Meredith's earrings was missing from my ear. I was on my hands and knees searching the backyard for it when I heard a voice.

"Bridge?"

I started, entirely shocked to find anyone outside with me—especially Liam.

"Yeah?" I said, my voice scratchy. I looked up to see him sitting on the settee on my patio.

He stood up, walked over to me and crouched down to my level.

"What are you…uh, what are you doin'?" He sounded like he was talking to a child he was babysitting but wasn't entirely comfortable with.

"My earring?" I was having trouble thinking of words, much less saying them.

"Did you lose it?"

I nodded. "I did."

He gave a light sigh. "All right, let's look for it then. Do you know that it's out here somewhere?"

I shook my head this time and started to stand. The heel on my shoe stuck in a crack between bricks, and I found myself on the ground again. Liam was instantly at my side, helping me up.

I felt nervous. Here it was. My moment to appear attractive to Liam, and I was sloppy smashed.

"Liam…"

"Y'all right, Bridget? Why don't you sit down."

"My earring—"

"I know." He helped me to the seat he'd just vacated.

"It looks like, um…an earring that's, uh. It's like a silver, sort of loops around…"

He laughed and knelt in front of me. I had no idea what he was doing, and then I felt him tuck my hair behind the ear that still had an earring. My head was spinning, and my heart was beating so hard I was sure he could hear it. I watched the smile fade as he shifted his gaze from my earring to my eyes.

I knew him so well, and yet he was rarely thinking what I thought he was. I'd never have guessed that that night so long ago, for example, he was going to break up with me. And at this moment, I didn't want to get my hopes up and think that maybe his heart was beating just as hard as mine.

I tried to look calm and collected as I felt his fingertips move down my neck. Then I felt the familiar ache of want and longing in my chest. The one I always felt when Liam was around.

A crease appeared between his eyebrows and he looked down at our hands, which until that moment I hadn't realized were entwined. Why? Why did he look like that? Was he regretting getting this close to me? Was it that he wanted me, but knew that he might have lost his chance?

Or maybe it was none of that, just that his knees were hurting from crouching down like this.

I watched his eyes move beneath his dark, straight eyelashes, and thought of all the times I'd looked into them and felt safety and relief.

I thought of the day at the pool that Liam had mentioned earlier. I'd knocked out my front tooth and lain pathetically on the side of the pool, crying from the pain and (mostly) the embarrassment. He had kneeled on the hot concrete next to me and asked if I was okay, moving my wet hair from my face just as he'd done again just now.

I missed the earliest days with him. My whole life, even in middle school and into high school, when I began to measure my happiness by how many "friends" I had, had always been better when he was there. He was the person in my life who knew me the best, and who was more interested in the side of me that knew every word to every Disney movie than the side of me that could tell you what was "wrong" with the outfit of every girl I knew. Being around him had always felt like taking a deep breath.

It felt the same way now.

After trying too hard all night long to regain the popularity I'd been so sure was the most important thing about me, being around Liam felt as easy as it always had. I always felt like…more around him. Like maybe I could be more if I was just with him. But I couldn't be that girl, the one who depended on a guy that way.

I sighed and leaned into the hand he had moved around to cup my cheek.

"I'm so tired of being like this, Liam." Once I said it, I felt ashamed. It was one of those drunken ramblings you regret in the morning.

"Like what?" He looked questioningly at me, melting me once again with his familiar gaze.

I thought carefully about my words.

"It's…hard to say, I don't know. I feel like every day is a struggle to keep my life the way it's been for however long. And I think…" I wrinkled my forehead, trying to put it the right way "…that it's so I'm happy. But I'm not really very happy with who I am or how my life is or…whatever." I tilted my head at him. "Am I?"

A quick smile flitted across his face as he pulled his hand away from mine.

"I'm not saying anything right," I slurred. "I think it was the tequila. I don't even *like* to drink!" I put my hands up in the air as if to say "go figure!"

"That makes five of us," he said, and upon seeing my confused expression, he elaborated. "You, me, Michelle, Jillian and…" he hesitated for half an instant "…Anna."

I stiffened upon the reminder of Anna and let out a dramatic exclamation.

I didn't want to think about her. It felt like being sure you'd almost talked your way out of jail and then having the guard lock up and say good-night.

"Right. Five of us." I stood again, still unsteady. He took me by the waist and hooked an arm under my knees. After a brief moment of batting his arm away and failing, I leaned into his warm body and allowed him to pick me up, letting out a quiet "Okay, let's go."

"Come on, cliché drunk girl, let's get you to your bed."

I laughed, not thinking of anything except how nice it was to feel like *us* even for this brief moment. That feeling of us-ness had disappeared so quickly after we broke up. We had once been so close, and then all of a sudden it was…gone. And we had to pretend it never happened.

I reveled in the feeling, pretending that we'd never split.

When Liam deposited me onto my bed, I felt the smallest flicker of hope that he might stay with me. That maybe we'd stay up all night talking like we used to (back when I had something interesting to say), and go out to the field and watch the sky's color change from night to dawn again.

I felt sure I could set aside my exhaustion.

"Liam…" I said, putting a hand on his forearm. I pulled on him, and he sat down next to me, his feet on the floor, and turned so that he could see me.

I couldn't see his face. He was just a silhouette in the light that poured in from the hallway. "Yeah, B?"

A chill ran through me as he called me that. He was the only one who *ever* called me that.

"Do you ever miss me?"

His shadowy figure shifted. "I do miss you."

I tightened my grip on his arm at the words, and then we were silent for a moment. He leaned over to me, and ran his fingers through my hair. I opened my mouth to say more, not knowing what I'd end up saying, but closed it when he stood.

He pulled my shoes off and laid my blankets on top of me. Suddenly I was awake again. I wanted to cry. I wanted to beg him to stay with me.

"You all right, Bridget?" he asked, stopping on his way to the door.

All I could do was nod, feeling like a little girl.

I felt sick. Though it seemed likely that it was from drinking too much, it felt more to do with Liam being here and my not being able to keep him. I wanted to tell him I could be me again, but why would he believe me? I didn't know if I could be.

Here I was, my mouth tasting like swill-soaked cotton, and even with my eyes shut it felt like the darkness was moving like the rollers on a slot machine. I wasn't just sleepy. I was passing out. Suddenly I missed the innocence of those summer days when the most I had before bed was a Coke and the worst I had when waking up was a hard time deciding whether to go to the pool or Michelle's house. Now I was just a fool of a girl who spent her time trying hard to be cool. Not the best. Not the smartest. Just…the most powerful.

The thought shook me, and made me feel like I was growing up too soon. Not that tonight had been mature in any way at all.

Tears built in my throat. I wanted to cry for the loss of him, the loss of myself and the loss of innocence.

"'K." I didn't want him to see what I was feeling. I tried to sound in control of everything, but ended up over-pronouncing all of my words. "I'll see you on Monday then."

"Monday," he agreed. "You'll be okay 'til then?"

"I'm fine," I lied. How could anyone believe me, the way I garbled it?

But he did.

Maybe he just wanted to.

He left, and for the few minutes that I spent conscious, I imagined where he was going. I hoped against hope that he'd go straight home, without Anna. I pictured her approaching him, like the easy girl in movies, and him holding up a hand to say "Halt, harlot!"

I fell asleep, slipping into the kind of dreams

that aren't dreams at all—just memories with all the details you never thought you'd remember and couldn't believe you'd forgotten.

# CHAPTER SIX

I woke up the next morning with a palpitating heartbeat and an overall feeling of fragility. It seemed like anything could tip me over the edge and make me throw up. I stayed in bed with the TV on until 6:00 p.m., drifting in and out of consciousness.

The room might have spun all day, and my head might have pounded, but nothing could have been worse than going into the kitchen for graham crackers and Coke and seeing—through unfocused eyes—Anna and Meredith sitting at my table. Together. In my kitchen.

Please tell me this was me drifting out of consciousness, and into a nightmare.

I was wearing my scruffy terry cloth robe and

mismatched socks, which went well with my bird's nest of a hairdo and face streaked with mascara from sideways tears I'd apparently cried in my sleep. So to stumble around the corner and see the perfectly styled heads of the two of *them*...I thought I might just need to find a gun. I wasn't sure yet which of us to use it on.

"What are you—" I started to ask why Anna was there, but realized Meredith wasn't supposed to be home yet, either. "Why is either of you here?"

Meredith looked at me. My heart stopped as I remembered the mess I hadn't thought to clean up the night before.

"I came home early because your father was too busy." Something flickered in her face that I was too confused to wonder about. "But I can't believe you!" she exclaimed.

My heart stopped. I scrambled to think of an excuse for all the bottles and cans that must be strewn all over the porch.

"I didn't think you'd be home yet, I just—"

Anna coughed, and pushed a stray hair from her face.

"It's no big deal, Mrs. Duke. Honestly, I only waited a few minutes."

What the hell was she talking about? I squinted my eyes at Anna.

"Oh, Anna, that's nice of you to say, but it was completely inconsiderate of her to sleep through her plans with you."

I looked at Anna, who was smiling. Yes, the gun was to be used on her.

"Well, I probably should head out anyway." She looked at me. "You don't look like you're feeling all that well, so we'll just hang out another time, okay?"

I watched in a daze as Anna told Meredith how nice it was to meet her, as Meredith agreed, and as they kissed the air next to each other's cheeks.

Well, that's just sarcastic.

I chased Anna out to her car to ask her what the *hell* was going on. My robe billowed in the wind like some kind of ridiculous cape, and my slippers flapped around on the driveway.

"What was *that* all about?"

"Don't worry about it," she said, coolly. "I came back after driving some of your friends home and cleaned up the mess from last night. I assumed you didn't want her to know about the drinking, and I was right in assuming you'd be in no condition to clean it all up. I'm just lucky I got here before she did."

I stared angrily at her before spitting out, "Well, then. Thanks."

I started up the front stairs and ignored her advice to take a cold shower.

For the rest of the evening, I worked myself into a depression. Anna was here, taking over. She was undoing all the work I'd done. She was moving in on my territory, and suddenly I wasn't the person I was at least *comfortable* being anymore. My power was failing.

It wasn't my imagination. That much I knew. People listened to me and did what I asked, things worked out for me whether the reason was luck or flirting, and I'd been perfectly content with that for a long time. Sure, sometimes it felt like I had only fans and no friends… but that'd been fine for a long time.

My life had changed somehow, and very abruptly. But maybe things would be back to normal soon.

WHEN I WOKE UP ON MONDAY morning, I was wearing the same pajamas I'd worn the whole day before. And when I headed to the bathroom to put on my makeup, I felt tired of my reflection.

Once I'd finished putting on the same makeup I put on every day, I glared at myself. Something was different about me. Something had changed to make the makeup seem empty and mask-like.

I got to school early (a first) and when I walked into Mr. Ezhno's classroom, I saw that almost everyone was gathered around Jillian. She had her lips tightened, the way she did when she was pretending to zip her lips so she wouldn't tell a secret.

"...and her *stepmom?*" asked one of the girls in the crowd, incredulously. I didn't remember her name.

Another girl I didn't know spotted me and said, "Shh" to the rest of them. *Shh* might as well have meant *she's here!*

They all went back to their seats, tossing glances at me. Each of them seemed to think they were being subtle.

So then the answer to my question would be, No, things are not going to go back to normal.

"What?" I said, feeling stupid and awkward. It seemed so obvious that they'd been talking about me, but for some reason I still didn't feel the complete vindication I should have felt by confronting them. It seemed presumptuous to assume the gossip was about me.

"Nothing, we just thought you were Mr. Ezhno." It was Logan who spoke this time. Logan, who used to sit in the back and talk about how hot I was, but now apparently had taken up lying badly.

“How could any of you possibly think I was Mr. Ezhno? That doesn’t even make—”

I was stopped short by Mr. Ezhno himself walking through the door and knocking into me.

“Oh, I’m sorry, Miss Duke.” He bent to pick up the pile of papers he’d dropped during our collision. “It’s just so weird to see you *in* the classroom, I suppose.”

There was a swell of whispers and snickering in the room. I headed to my seat, observing more “subtle” looks that were shot my way.

I felt the familiar shame flow through my bloodstream. I hadn’t felt this way since middle school. I couldn’t control what was happening around me.

Matt Churchill raised his hand as soon as attendance had been called.

“So what did *you* do this weekend, Mr. Ezhno?”

Mr. Ezhno narrowed his eyes, and I knew he was just as curious as I about the reason for the giggles that were still filling the classroom.

“I worked on progress reports, which I have here, actually...” He waved the pile of papers he’d just cleaned up and started handing them out.

“Yeah, what else did you do?” said Logan, clearly

speaking for Matt, who was laughing too hard to speak.

What the hell was so funny? It seemed like the only two people left in the dark were Mr. Ezhno and myself. Since when was I a) in a category with *him* or b) left in the dark about anything?

Mr. Ezhno hesitated before looking irritatedly at the ceiling.

"I had a parent-teacher meeting, and then I took my son to the—"

The laughing became uproarious upon the mention of the meeting. I stared at him in disbelief, shocked that he would do such a thing as to bring it up.

He was talking about me, and it was really obvious. He was blatantly referencing my insubordination and the resulting steps taken to amend my "behavior."

I thought of the last time I'd been present at one of the conferences. Meredith had been all "John—I mean, Mr. Ezhno and I only want the best for you…" and every time *he* said anything, she'd nod silently and solemnly. It was enough to make anyone sick.

I looked at Mr. Ezhno. What a sight he was with his ugly plaid shirt and pleated pants. My lip curled in disgust as I watched him try fruitlessly to regain control over his class. Everyone was going to *know* whose parent he was talking about because I was, as Meredith had put it, the biggest "nuisance."

My fury grew as I realized that this must have been why everyone was talking about me. That's what the muttering about my stepmother was all about.

I sat there, mortified, for the rest of the class period, not knowing what my next move should be. Who was I supposed to take action against? What should I say?

I knew I was mad at Jillian for letting anything slip, I was mad at Mr. Ezhno for the same and I was mad at the class for laughing. But how do you tell thirty people at once to stop making fun of you?

Furthermore, how do you do that without sounding like one of the misfit toys from that old Christmas movie?

I decided that the best I could do was ignore Jillian. Which was hard, because she seemed to be ignoring me.

When class ended I dashed out of the classroom, the same way I'd done for years.

When I got to gym class, Michelle was acting much the same as Jillian had been, a discovery that really upset me. She'd been my last real hope of solidarity. I tried to talk to her, but all I got were obviously irritated, tight-lipped responses.

It was like there was something in the air. Something that made me some kind of leper. I walked through the hallways, feeling like a character in a movie where everyone is talking about you and pointing. And for most of the day, that's how it was.

But after a while it wasn't even that; I wasn't even getting *that* much attention. Some people were pointing or talking, but the rest of them just ignored me. I even had to move out of the way of some of them, I realized with a small shock. In the game of hallway chicken, I *always* won. Not something I'd really been doing on purpose, but certainly something I was noticing now.

I felt like a ghost. Not even a ghost—at least people were scared of or interested in ghosts. And if I were dead, the only difference would be that they'd be talking about me in full voices instead of whispers.

For the next few days, my life swirled downward more and more. In high school, the classes and days are like dog years. If you have a bad class, it's like having a bad week. And I may as well have been drudging through the mud of anonymity for months.

Suddenly it seemed that it wasn't just *me* who didn't recognize me anymore. It was everyone.

No texts, no calls, no guys asking me out, no one even *acknowledging* me at school, it seemed, no one asking me to play board games at their house. Eventually, no one was even talking *about* me, as far as I could tell.

My friends were all busy, and at lunch they talked only to each other, making me feel like a third wheel at my own table.

It felt like every day I woke up, went to school and then just waited to fall asleep again. No days had any value.

And it was pissing me off.

It's not even like I had some kind of strong family unit to depend on. Meredith was obviously no use, and my dad hadn't been home in forever. And really, what kind of consoling was he even capable of?

I spent those days working myself into an angry frenzy, thinking of everything that had happened. Everything that had happened to me.

One of my greatest abilities was to shove any blame entirely from myself, until ultimately I'd ridded myself of any guilt or responsibility.

So that's what I did. Whether I was conscious of it or not at the time. Everything became what *they* had done to *me*.

Mr. Ezhno had sent me to the office because he was too big a pansy to handle me on his own.

Brett shouldn't have ripped the paper—it was the *reason* we got caught. It was his own damn fault he was getting in trouble.

As for Jillian and Michelle? They were being awful, catty girls. Who needed them?

So when the next Thursday rolled around, I thought I'd set my plan into action. I was going to be myself again.

For the first half of the day I looked forward to lunch, hoping to get a chance to talk to Jillian and Michelle and figure out exactly what the deal was. I was halfway through the entrance to the cafeteria when I saw that Michelle, Jillian, Liam and Anna were sitting together. There was an empty seat, but it couldn't have been clearer that I was not welcome at the table. It was exactly as if Anna had replaced me.

Maybe not even that. The scene I was looking at could have existed if I had never gone to the school, if I wasn't there yet, if I'd come and gone, or as it was now—as if I just wasn't part of it.

And yet, in some way, it couldn't have existed without me. They were all in each other's realms because of me.

Then my self-pity and embarrassment transformed into absolute wrath.

I pounded off to the nearest bathroom, loathing the people at school. How *dare* they, I thought, how dare they whisper about me, cast me out, or ignore me?

I thought bitterly of Michelle and Jillian. Michelle had gotten all mad at me for no reason at my house on Saturday, and Jillian—well, Jillian was just willing to be friends with whoever told her what to do. I realized with a start that they, too, had known about the meeting between Meredith and Mr. Ezhno. Between my two best friends and my least favorite teacher, they were ruining my reputation.

But for neither of them to even *say* anything to me? What fake people.

What *bitches!*

Once in the bathroom, I locked myself in a stall and slammed down the top of the seat. I hung my bag on the hook and slumped down onto the seat, my heart beating hard.

I thought of all the rumors I'd spread. They'd all been much worse than a few parent-teacher conferences, and yet this seemed to be such a big deal. And it really wasn't.

Was that *really* what this was all about? It seemed strange that so many people would get so opinionated about my behavioral issues, which they had previously been entertained by.

I was just thinking of how much I despised Ezhno and his class when I heard his name called over the P.A. system.

*"John Ezhno, please report to the main office, John Ezhno, please report to the main office."*

*Please, God, let him be fired,* I thought to myself.

I looked to my right and read some of the writing on the wall, which I usually ignored.

Maybe this will cheer me up, I mused, thinking that reading smack talk about other people just might be the thing.

Mrs. Templeton's class is a JOKE her ass needs to lay off the COKE.

Rhyming, nice. Good that Mother Goose had had an impact on the restroom literature.

Nance Le Bloe needs to keep her legs shut.

True. She was a skank.

LIAM IS A SEXY BEAST.

A foul expression, but not untrue.

My eyes scanned the wall, which named a lot of girls as sluts and a lot of guys as hot, as well as a lot of teachers as jerks. I agreed with most all of them.

Hell, I could have written some of them.

I thought of writing something about Anna and then reconsidered.

I didn't have a pen.

There were a lot of words spelled wrong, and pointless things that I couldn't puzzle out like: judith was here. Why commemorate your bathroom trip that way, or even at all? I considered, amusedly, of adding *long enough to find a pen and write this.*

I looked on the opposite wall and saw even more. But that's when I saw the truly awful comments.

About me.

My heart sank as I read. I was a slut, I was a bitch, I was a spoiled brat and I was a lot of other things. I gasped audibly when I saw that someone even called me a c★★★, a word I had completely banned from my vocabulary, finding it to be one of the only truly offensive words.

I sat there, in shock, trying to wrap my head around this array of insults. Since when did people think I was *any* of those things? I'd never seen these comments before, and they all looked darker and fresher than the other accusations written there.

My vision turned blurry, and my ears rang as rage coursed through my bloodstream. I hated these girls, suddenly. How *dare* they talk about me that way? And how dare they put it on the walls like this? I didn't know what to do, whom to yell at, who to confide in about how much this really *hurt*—I didn't know anything except that I had to get out of here.

I pulled my bag from the hook and behind it found my name in big, bold, shiny letters I couldn't believe I'd missed before.

BRIDGET DUKE IS A LOSER AND EVERYONE KNOWS IT.

I WENT TO MY POST-LUNCH class and sat quietly in my seat for a few minutes, fighting back my emotions. I wasn't sure how they'd come out, whether I was going to uncharacteristically start punching people, or whether I was going to start sobbing.

Not long into the class, I excused myself and went to the health office. I shouldn't have to sit in class while my life fell apart.

As soon as I walked in, the nurse rolled her eyes at me before sending me into the back. I grimaced. Like it was up to her to judge me for coming in too often.

I chose the last cot, away from the moaning of an *actually* sick girl. I lay down on the faux-leather bed, which was always comfortable merely because it was a bed at school and not a gym exercise, and stared up at the speckled white ceiling tiles.

Earlier, my feelings had been pure anger and contempt for everyone I knew. I felt those feelings grow into desperation as I realized what exactly it was that was upsetting me so much.

Nobody cared about me.

The only person who didn't seem to be mad at me was my father. But he, I thought, dragging myself deeper into my feeling of anguish, didn't even care enough to be home. It wasn't that he wasn't mad at me; it was that he didn't care at all. He'd rather follow sports around the country and hotel-hop.

If my mother were here everything would be different. Everything would be better. If she hadn't died… well, it was just so unfair I couldn't even stand to think about it. I pushed the thought from my mind, just as I had done when she died.

I was told I wasn't allowed to go to her funeral. Never seeing her in a casket left me with only the option to do my best to block out the few memories I had of her last weeks. She'd been quiet and seemed angry in those days, and that's not how I wanted to remember her. But it had been so many years now since her death, and I'd been so young at the time that I hardly knew what was real anymore.

At the moment, I felt sure that if she hadn't died, my life would be a hundred times better than it was right now.

I continued to conjure up awful memories and reasons why no one cared about me.

The banana incident in elementary school.

When my father told me my mother wasn't coming back.

The time I'd had to take the rap for the Outdoor Ed incident even though it wasn't my fault.

Meredith tattling on me about the incident.

My father always leaving or spending all of his time at home with Meredith or alone, telling me he was too tired to talk to me.

And then the thing that had felt so on-the-surface lately: the five-minute span of time with Liam, in which we went from happily watching one of my favorite movies to being in the past tense.

It was the same thing I did when I cried and looked at myself in the mirror, just to see how pitiful and helpless I could really look.

Once I started thinking about my life in that light, it wasn't hard to keep going. I analyzed the things people had said to me over the last year or two, things I'd assumed were caused by jealousy.

The bathroom walls.

The whispering.

And the ignoring.

My face twisted into the expression that unhappy clown face paint is modeled after. I squeezed my eyes shut and wished as hard as I could for an answer. For something that could fix it all.

A moment later, I sat up, the tears that raced down my cheeks feeling cool on my hot, angry skin. The next thing I knew, I'd left school without signing out.

I practically ran to my car, where I sat for a moment, trying to calm down. I stared at the car's logo in the center of the steering wheel, thinking only of how angry I was.

My rage repeatedly brought me to the point of action, before I realized again and again that there was nothing I could do. This wasn't one girl who'd called me a slut who I could get revenge on by getting ahold of the P.A. microphone and announcing that her mother was here with her Ex-Lax. Because that, I thought with the smallest sensation of pride, I knew how to handle quite easily.

But no, this was different.

My thoughts were too self-pitying and hate-filled for me to calm down. What I needed was to get home.

I turned my key in the ignition and peeled out of my parking space. I knew it was dangerous to drive when I was so upset and barely able to see out of my blurry eyes. *But who cares,* I thought—if I crashed they'd all realize how much I meant to them.

As the thought flitted through my mind, I realized how petty and small of me it was to think that way. Not just that, but how screwed *up* it was to be that person.

But of course you know what happens next, because that's where we began. What you don't know is that I truly thought it would be the answer to all of my problems.

And in a way, it was.

# CHAPTER SEVEN

I woke up with that feeling you get when you're staying in a hotel room or at a friend's house as a kid and there's that moment where you're not sure where you are. But the more I awoke, the more I realized I didn't know where I was.

I was lying on my back, trying to open my eyes. It wasn't too bright in the room, but my eyes kept rolling back and my eyelids fluttered closed involuntarily, as if I was trying to look straight into the sun. I opened them into slits, but all I could see was a dark, wooden ceiling. My eyes closed again.

I was confused, but my exhaustion made me feel passive.

The first thing I felt was relief; at least I was here,

wherever I was. I was thinking and breathing. That meant I was alive, right?

The second thing I felt was fear. Maybe I wasn't alive; I mean, it's not like anyone knows what happens after you die, anyway. I started to panic as I imagined what might be happening to me.

One option was that I had been in a coma for thirty years. But, I amended, who would keep me plugged in that long?

Maybe I was in a hospital, the crash only a few hours behind me.

I tried to pull myself into a sitting position, but my body was too sore. I thought with a cringe of the last moments in my car. What was wrong with me?

More thoughts rushed into my head: the betrayals of my friends, the fact that few (if any) people loved or cared about me, the fact that everyone was too focused on themselves to think a little bit about what they were doing to me.

And Anna. Stupid Anna Judge had to come along and ruin everything. And how, I asked myself furiously, *how* did she do it? Before she came to school a week ago—assuming I wasn't waking up from a multiple-decade coma—everything was fine. No one hated me, no one was mad at me, no one was stupid enough to talk about me behind my back. Not only that, but they actually liked me. People had thought I was funny, guys checked me out when I walked by and people listened to what I said.

Now everyone was friends with Anna. Everyone thought *she* was so beautiful and impressive. Hell, even at my very own party everyone was only interested in me until she showed up.

How's that for a walking, talking slap in the face?

I tried to refocus my thoughts back to the more pressing matter—what was happening now.

When I strained to sit up again, my entire body shook the way unused muscles do when used for strenuous work. I finally got myself up, and realized I was lying in the middle of a huge…table? I rubbed my eyes, which were still hard to keep open, and looked toward my feet. Empty chairs surrounded the table. A boardroom?

Of all the scenarios in which I thought I might find myself, a boardroom was not on the list.

Suddenly, someone spoke behind me.

"If you've finished with your nap, we'd like to get started."

I gasped and turned quickly to see who it was.

No way.

*"Anna?"*

She gave a smug smile and splayed her arms in a gesture that said, "None other."

Fear ran up and down my spine. The situation kept making less and less sense.

But she wasn't the only one there. I looked at the group of people sitting at that end of the table. Liam, Michelle, Meredith, Mr. Ezhno and Brett. I breathlessly said each of the names, but no one looked at me except for Anna. They were all flipping through yellow legal pads.

At least Liam was there. The situation couldn't be too terrifying if Liam was involved.

"What is going on here?" I said, twisting my aching body onto my knees, my eyes on Liam. I lost a bit of the bite to my question during an awkward moment spent cautiously lowering myself to my feet. "And what do you mean, 'get started?' Get started with what? I was in my car, and now I'm in a boardroom. I have *no* idea what is happening."

I was feeling a little hysterical.

"I realize that. Which is why we need to get started." Anna smiled and sat back a little in her chair, her hands crossed neatly on the table. Her calmness was making me even more uneasy.

I hated not being in control of what was happening to me. It had been my problem even when I was a little girl. If I wasn't sure where I was, or if I wasn't fully aware of what was happening around me, I panicked. If I lost track of my mother in a department store, I'd be found in the middle of a clothing rack, weeping. It had happened more than once.

I looked at the people in front of me. I was breathing hard, watching them. None of them even tossed a glance my way.

"Michelle." No reply. "Michelle, I'm serious, answer me." What the hell was *with* her recently?

She didn't move.

"Liam? Liam, please." I begged him to answer me, or at the very least to respond in some way. A blink, anything.

Nothing.

"Meredith?" Even when Meredith was mad at me, she would never ignore me.

I looked to Anna for an explanation.

She just shook her head regretfully.

"I'm sorry, Bridget, it's not the time for that right now." I could tell she wasn't going to say any more on the subject of the others.

I took in the room surrounding me. All of the walls

were a deep, rich mahogany. Nothing hung from them and there were no windows. I turned to look behind me.

"No, you won't find a door," Anna said, watching me impassively.

I shook my head. "All right, enough. This is a weird and stupid joke. It is not funny now, and it's not something we'll all laugh about later, so let's just stop it before it goes any further."

"You're right, Bridget," Anna said. I took a second to be surprised by how easily she'd given up, and by the fact that this was a joke. But then she continued. "It wouldn't be a funny joke. And I assure you that no one here thinks this is funny."

I studied her face, looking for some indication of dishonesty or humor. There was none. Just complete conviction.

"Okay, this is ridiculous. I don't even *know* you. And I seriously don't want to end up on CNN because you went nutso and killed me."

"You don't want to die anymore, then?"

"I never—" My gut lurched. "What do you mean by *that?*"

"Tell us what your thoughts were as you drove home from school, won't you?"

I stared at her. How did she know about that? She couldn't. She must have guessed.

"That was an accident, I didn't mean to crash."

Anna smiled and clearly seemed to be thinking, *If that's what you have to tell yourself…*

Perhaps she was crazy.

Perhaps *I* was. That was seeming more likely by the second.

I stood carefully, trying to not let the pain or fear I was feeling deter me from my mission. I creaked over to the wood panel nearest me. I pushed, and instantly felt like a fool. Anna had started looking through her own notepad, and the others still wouldn't look at me. I pushed on the next wall, then the next, until I'd pushed on every wall but one. Finally I walked over to it, banking all of my hope on it.

"This can't…I—this is a dream, right? Some easily interpreted dream that I'll understand in the morning?"

I felt stupid for saying it. People who *weren't* in dreams, and who asked if they were…well, that would be called *insane.*

Anna said nothing. She merely stared at me benevolently.

My mind started to spin with anger, the result of feeling foolish and hopelessly trapped. Because I had to try, I pushed on the final wall. A swear word escaped my throat and my heart began to hammer against my chest as I realized that wherever I was, whatever was happening, I was stuck.

There was no way out.

I walked over to a chair a few down from Liam. I kept my eyes on him, studying his features, which looked so fixated on whatever he was reading.

"All right, let's get started." Anna organized the papers in front of her and picked up a yellow legal pad and a pen. "First of all, is there anything you'd like to say?" Her tone was now all business, kindness gone.

All I could do was shake my head.

"Just as I thought." She wrote something down. "All right, then let me ask you another question. What common threads are there between these five people?" She indicated the group that flanked her.

"I don't know," I said, breathing tentatively. "Obviously we all know each other."

"Okay. And do you have any idea why they might all be here to talk to you at this time?"

The first answer that came to my mind was that I had been in an accident and they were all here because they love me, but something told me that *none* of these people were here out of love.

Not if they wouldn't even look at me.

So I thought for a moment about her question, but truthfully didn't have any idea what might bring all of these people to a boardroom in wherever we were. I still didn't even know what brought *me* here.

I spared her these thoughts and shook my head once more.

"All right. One last thing." She leaned back in her chair. "Would you consider yourself to be popular, Bridget?"

Something about the way she asked the question made me sure that she didn't consider that to be the case. But I sat up a little straighter, and said that I did. She scribbled something else onto her pad of paper.

"And if you don't mind my asking, how did that come about?"

I found that question odd. Most people probably wouldn't have an answer. But I, as it happened, did.

It had really begun at the start of eighth grade, when my only three friends got expelled.

The exact reason *why* they were expelled was never fully explained to the general student body. All we knew was that it was bad.

The funny thing was, they'd told me in no uncertain terms that I was not allowed to participate in the prank.

After they were caught, I realized I was alone in school. I spent the next summer terrified of going into eighth grade without any friends.

When the first day of school finally came, I was exceedingly pleased to find that everyone was being nice to me. Boys were flirting with me, girls were timidly asking if I was headed the same way as they were to class, or asking if the seat next to me was taken at lunch. I didn't understand any of it at first, until Jillian—whom I did not know at the time—sat down with me in the library during one of our classes. She talked about normal things at first, asking me if I hated the project we were working on, too, and who I had a crush on (a question I had responded to with a blush as Liam's face drifted into my mind). Finally, after a furtive glance at another table, she mentioned the prank the other three girls had pulled at the end of the last school year. Judging by the eager-looking girls watching our conversation, it seemed that Jillian was the only one with the guts enough to ask me about it.

I shook my head shyly and said that I really didn't want to talk about it. That I didn't know any more than they did. I remember feeling disappointed as I realized that that was why she'd sat with me; it wasn't because she liked me. But then she looked at me with the widest of eyes, and asked me how on earth I'd gotten away with it.

And that was the second that it all made sense.

I was the only one remaining of the four. *I* was the one everyone was scared of. None of them seemed to know that I'd just been along for the ride with that group, that I had never come up with ideas to terrorize my peers. No one knew that my constant "I don't think we should do this" and crying were the reason I hadn't been allowed to hang out with the group anymore and the reason I wasn't let in on the prank that got them kicked out. They didn't know anything about it.

And, given the fact that their fear made me their leader, I wasn't going to be the one to tell them.

Once I realized what had happened, I took the opportunity to be a proud but fair leader. I was nice to everyone, eager to maintain my newfound status. I never again wanted to feel I wasn't one hundred percent in control.

It wouldn't be until later that I knowingly began to abuse that power.

I kept all of this awareness to myself, however, and chose not to share it with Anna. Why was I going to tell her anything? She was doing a pretty crappy job of answering *my* questions.

Instead, I just shrugged. "I guess it just happened."

After a long moment, in which I felt sure she knew everything I had just remembered, Anna brought her eyebrows together like she was thinking very hard about something.

"Hmm." She put the notepad down on the table and stood. "There are a few things that I'd like you to see."

"What kind of things?"

"Please stand."

"Are we going somewhere? I thought there weren't any doors," I said, feeling fooled.

I was surprised to see that she was wearing something that looked like a judge's cloak. Not only was this weird—she was dressing for her name?—but I was usually the first one to notice another girl's outfit.

She looked at the ground in front of my feet. I followed her gaze and saw a pair of Adidas. I didn't know what she was getting at.

"...What?"

"Step in."

"Step—what, into the shoes?"

She nodded. I lifted a foot to step in, and then felt idiotic and stopped.

*"Really?"* I asked.

Anna said nothing, but the command in her silence was clear. I lifted my foot again and stepped into the left shoe, looking self-consciously around me, though I knew I had no attentive audience.

"Fine. I'll play your stupid little game. But I swear, if I'm being Punk'd right now..."

"You have to be a celebrity to be Punk'd."

I gave a single nasty laugh and then took my second step into the other well-worn shoe. The second I did, I felt like Alice falling down the rabbit hole.

My eyes were shut and I couldn't open them. I tried to scream but the sound seemed very far away. It felt like wearing someone else's glasses, with the dizziness and inability to perceive space. There was a ringing in my ears that reminded me of how I'd felt at camp one year when I fainted from the heat.

Then, all of a sudden, it stopped.

When I could finally see again, I found myself in another room. But this time, I recognized it.

## CHAPTER EIGHT

I was crouched down in the corner of the cloakroom in my fifth-grade classroom. My body felt small and compact, fitting in the corner quite snugly. I could hear a child's voice in the next room saying, "Heads down, thumbs up!"

On my lap there was a piece of pink construction paper with a pencil-drawn heart in the middle. I watched my hand writing in loopy, slanted cursive, but I couldn't control it. I looked at the words that appeared on the page. *And without you, this place would be…*

I had a split second of dawning, uncertain comprehension before I heard footsteps coming into the room.

I looked up to see my very favorite light-up Little

Mermaid sneakers come squeaking into the room in front of me.

*I was in Brett's body.* Holy—this was no joke.

I was feeling everything he felt, understanding everything he thought and doing everything he did, but I had no control. It was like watching a TV show from inside one of the characters while having an intense understanding of another character.

A stab of foreboding hit me before I heard the ten-year-old Bridget Duke speak.

"Brett!"

The paper was snatched from my lap and I watched myself—across from me—read it, all the while feeling the fear that Brett had been feeling.

I watched the girl's face, my face, and saw my eyes scan the poem. Watched as my eyebrows furrow as I came upon words I didn't know or recognize.

Everything went dark as Brett burrowed his face in his hands very suddenly.

*No, no, no, no, NO!* I knew what I was going to do, and I could feel that ten-year-old Brett had known also.

I looked up to see my own face burst into a victorious smile. The next thing I saw was my ponytail swinging out of the cloakroom.

I heard my voice in the next room singing "Brett loves Miche-elle!"

My new stomach dropped, I felt embarrassment flood into Brett. I heard my voice reading the poem aloud, using a nasty tone that made all of the words sound dirty. I listened as the rest of the class joined into the guffawing I remembered creating.

And then, in unison, everyone sang the K-I-S-S-I-N-G song.

Brett stood shakily, kicking the other papers out of his path, and crept over to the wall to peer into the classroom. His gaze locked on Michelle.

I felt his surge of relief as he realized she wasn't laughing. She didn't look amused at all. In fact, she looked downright embarrassed. The relief he felt to see that she wasn't laughing at him combined with his empathy for how she must be feeling. The fondness for her was so strong that I felt, for a moment, Brett's urge to run up to her and tell her how sorry he was.

He was barely even thinking about his own shame.

Deciding that it would only make things worse for her if he did run over, Brett headed to his backpack.

He gathered up the papers from the ground, the scissors, his multi-colored pencil (part of a set that had his name on it) and the tape, and threw all of it into the big section of his bag. Hoisting it onto his shoulder, he stormed out of the room. I could feel the humiliation and the longing to be home all the way to my core.

Memories of his family and a home that I'd never seen before flittered through Brett's mind. With each memory his pace quickened, until finally he burst full speed into the main office.

He looked around for Mrs. Gibbs, one of the secretaries. When she came out of the copier room, she looked pleased to see Brett. It was peculiar, because in *my* recollection, she'd been a disdainful woman who did little more than frown at students.

"Hi, Brett!" she said.

Brett felt a distinct comfort upon seeing her. "Hi, Mrs. Gibbs."

Her cheer faded a little, as she looked at his face. "Are you feeling sick?"

"Not…exactly. Something just happened in class and…"

It was then that she seemed to take in what Brett was feeling. "Oh, no," she said, her freckled arms dropping to her sides, "don't tell me it's that Bridget Duke again."

Ex*cuse* me? "That" Bridget Duke? *Again?*

Brett nodded, and my stomach tightened. It was like

eavesdropping, except that I was sure to not get caught. And I didn't want to hear what she had to say about me.

"You know, that girl is going to hear it from me one day. The number of students she's terrorized into going home early and put in the guidance office, I swear." She sat down in the chair behind her desk. "What did she do this time, Brett?"

"I was writing a valentine to Michelle, and then she caught me and read it to the whole class. Everyone laughed at me." I felt Brett's mortification swell again.

Mrs. Gibbs was shaking her head. "So mean. Someday, someone will tell her off, believe you me. If I wasn't—" She stopped, as if remembering that Brett was there and that whatever else she had to say wasn't appropriate for a child's ears. "Well, never mind that. Let's just call your mother, shall we?"

Brett nodded again, and watched as Mrs. Gibbs dialed his home number.

"Hi, Teresa? Yes, it's Sybil. Brett's here, and one of the other children hurt his feelings. He seems very upset—" She paused and nodded at the words Teresa was saying. "Mmm-hmm. It's unacceptable, certainly. Well, don't you worry about it, I'll excuse him in the system, and you just get here whenever you can. All right? It's always wonderful to talk to you, Teresa. Mmm-hmm. Buh-bye."

While they waited for Brett's mom to arrive, Mrs. Gibbs stopped herself short of saying a number of things to him, but her sympathetic glances spoke volumes to me.

He sat silently, not eager to make conversation.

When Brett's mother finally did come through the doors, the safety he felt was something I hadn't felt in a long time. I thought for a moment of how much I missed that particular brand of comfort. I wondered when the last time I'd really felt it was, and landed quickly on a memory of my own mother. Was that really the last time I'd felt it? That day we'd eaten cheese fondue and watched *The Sound of Music* during the rainstorm?

I was so lost in my own thoughts that I could hardly focus on Brett's. The thing that finally got me back to Brett's mind was when I felt him begin to cry.

I felt him shake with silent sobs and heard the echoing of my singsong voice in his head. The way I'd twisted his words and made them sound so foolish. The way I'd acted without concern for him or Michelle. Focused only on entertaining everyone else in order to benefit myself.

I remembered that day almost as clearly as I was feeling it now. I'd *wanted* to get back at Brett. He'd gotten an extra bag of candy for getting a math problem right. One that I'd gotten wrong. It had seemed like *such* a big deal at the time.

Brett's mother's arm was roped around him, trying to steady his shaking as she said quiet, soothing words about what they'd all do that night as a family. Movies, games and anything else Brett felt up to.

Resentment stabbed me as I thought of how incredibly unfair it was I had to be with someone else's mother in a flashback instead of going back far enough to see my own.

And then everything went dark again. I felt the dizziness and the nausea and the ringing all rush back to me, until I found myself face to face with—and it was weird—me.

The current me.

"—and, be real, when else are you going to have a chance with Michelle?" My voice sounded brash and overbearing to the ears I heard it through now.

I felt Brett's irritation with me rise as I said it was his only shot. He thought for a moment of how to explain why that was such an incredibly demeaning suggestion. Tried to put *unethical* into terms I might understand.

"It's not right, you can't just trade her like money or something."

Brett thought of Michelle. He was feeling something I'd felt so many times in my life. The desire to instantly go tell Michelle about whatever had just happened.

But why was *Brett* feeling that way?

"Here, just ask her to talk to me. I'll ask her out myself." A gush of smugness went through Brett, and I wondered again why he would be feeling anything remotely close to confidence when it came to Michelle.

"So we have a deal. She'll sit with you Monday at lunch." I watched myself walk away. Brett felt disgusted with me, and half wanted to just call the whole thing off for my presumption. I felt him wish he could tell me to get stuffed, that of course he wouldn't help me.

But a pang of loyalty coursed through him. It was an unfamiliar feeling for me.

I was surprised to see that he really disliked me. Deeply. Not that I didn't see that my actions were irksome, but it wasn't even that he hated me. I didn't intimidate him, he wasn't interested in me. He just *simply* did not like me.

The thought was darkly compelling.

Yet at the same time, part of him wanted to help me. That was the part I really didn't understand. If he felt this way about me, why not just tell me to screw off? Another image of Michelle floated through his mind, as he contemplated helping me.

What *is* that?

I had wondered where it was Brett had been going after that conversation, given that he was headed away from the cafeteria at the start of lunch. I was surprised to see him go straight to the NSL classroom and study.

For thirty long minutes Brett studied the material for the test, putting me in the miserable position of *having* to study for a test. I watched him go over and over the vocabulary words, forced to spend at least some of our mutual thoughts on the definitions.

The mousy substitute teacher came into the room, quietly acknowledging Brett before opening up her romance novel and waiting for everyone else to arrive.

When the students did start coming into the classroom, the distinct feeling of *thank God* rushed through my head. But as soon as *I* walked in, Brett's irritation with my very presence left no room in his head for my own thoughts.

"Hey, Brett?" It was unsettling to hear my voice. Just like listening to an answering machine recording of your voice and realizing that you sound almost exactly like Kermit the Frog.

"Yeah?" Brett stared down at his paper, barely listening, and working to memorize another definition.

"I talked to Michelle, and she's looking forward to Monday." I heard myself lie.

He fought back a smile. He actually felt like *laughing.*

Maybe Brett was insane, I considered.

While the substitute, Miss Smithson, introduced herself and handed out the papers, Brett continued to study. Even once he had to put his papers away, he kept running over the definitions and facts to himself.

I was exceedingly happy that I didn't always have to share a mind with Brett.

As soon as the test was on Brett's desk, he started filling it out in a frenzy to finish before the answers escaped from his mind.

"*Slow down!*" I heard my command from the next desk over.

Brett looked at me, angered by my cheek. Brett thought to himself, *She'll understand,* and decided that he wasn't going to help me to cheat. *She'll understand?* Why would he think that I would understand?

After a quick glance at the substitute, whose nose

was still in her book, he ripped the corner of the test off. The sub looked up, and Brett filled out the next answer on his test. Once we weren't Miss Smithson's focus anymore, Brett wrote the note to me. I can't do this. You have to do the work.

Brett kept his eyes on the paper, knowing that my reaction would be less than accepting. Sure enough, after the sound of the note being opened, there was a sharp intake of breath.

*"You. Have. To."* I heard my voice, which sounded harsh, but which I knew to be desperate.

"I can't. I can't risk it." It was true, Brett thought, it wasn't worth it to risk getting in trouble for Bridget. I hated the way he thought my name. Like he tagged "of all people" on the end of it.

Like it was a joke.

Brett hurried back to his test, trying to ignore any other comments I might make. Even *I* didn't want to hear me. I was being entirely annoying.

"Could you two please step out into the hall?"

I felt the panic from both my own memories of being caught, and Brett's. By the time we'd gotten out in the hall, Brett had already run through a slew of fears. None of them, incidentally, had been like mine. None were fear of a parent's wrath. The dominating emotion Brett seemed to be feeling was the fear of disappointing his parents.

"Cheating is an unacceptable act of behavior. I must say I am disappointed. Now which one of you wants to explain to me what happened?"

Brett thought carefully of how to make it seem like it wasn't a big deal. *Best that no one gets in trouble,* he thought. But before he could think of something innocent to say we'd been talking about, the inevitable came. I longed to stop the words from coming out of my mouth.

"I tried to tell him to stop, Miss Smithson. I know it's wrong to talk during a test, but I didn't know what else to do. I'm so sorry, Miss Smithson, really."

Brett stared at me. I could feel the ire building in his chest as he watched my bad attempt at sincerity.

"Brett, is this true?" Miss Smithson looked at Brett.

"I was trying to tell *her* not to cheat!"

The way he said it scared me just as it had before. Except this time I could feel it in his mind. The feeling of injustice overwhelming me. The fear that *that girl,* as Mrs. Gibbs had referred to me so many times, might get away with this kind of backward lie.

"You're either going to agree here on who it was, or you're both going to be punished to the full extent."

"I understand."

I watched my own smug face.

Brett's disinterest in confrontation was conflicting with his anger. If he spoke up, he was just going to look desperate. And he had no proof that he hadn't been cheating.

"See? You can see that it's his, because it's the corner of the first page on his test. See, he said he couldn't do it, and that I had to do the work. For him."

Brett's stomached plummeted from shock that I'd been able to turn this around so brilliantly.

When we were on the way to the office, Brett tried to find the loophole that would prove him innocent. Thoughts ran through his head of the colleges he was applying to, the grades he'd worked so hard to keep up, the disappointment he'd caused his parents during his brief period of silly rebellion. He thought of me. He thought of the trouble I had caused without any thought to anyone else.

"Listen, Brett—" I heard myself start to speak.

"Shut up, Bridget," Brett said. No explanation was going to work, and any apology—and he seemed sure there wouldn't be one anyway—wouldn't be enough.

Once in the office, Brett and I were told to sit in the waiting area. A moment after we sat down, the headmaster called for Bridget Duke. I watched myself stand up and walk into the office.

I winced inwardly as I thought of what I'd said in there. Of how I'd looked the headmaster dead in the eye and said how awful it was that Brett would do something like that. I'd said things about how appalling it was that Brett seemed to be slipping back into his old habits.

I spoke warily of how hard I'd studied for the test.

I had known even then that the headmaster was on to me. But he was in the unfortunate position of not being able to make character judgments.

After all, as far as he knew, what he'd been told were the facts. And I had the substitute on my side.

When I finally emerged from the office, Brett observed that I looked too pleased. I sauntered out, happy with myself for getting away with it. I felt Brett's anger as he watched me go.

"Brett?" The headmaster summoned him with a weary hand gesture.

Brett entered the office, closed the door behind him and sank into one of the high-backed leather armchairs.

Headmaster Ransic took off his glasses and buried his face in his hands. Brett felt uncomfortable as he watched him. After a long moment, the headmaster ran his fingers through his own hair and spoke.

"All right, Mr. Cooper. I know exactly what's going on here."

"What do you mean?" Brett said, cautious not to misunderstand that proclamation in the way that so many movie characters do.

"Now, correct me if I'm wrong, but this is a…fabrication of Miss Duke's, is it not?"

Brett gaped in the same way that I would have.

"I'm sorry, I don't know…"

"Mr. Cooper, I believe I know you moderately well at this point. I've advised you for a few years, and have certainly seen the transformation in your motivation. You've been in here at least once a week to pick up community service hours. I've seen your grade point average move up from the 1.0 in your freshman year to what it is now. I know that you're trying. I have also watched Miss Duke do—" he searched for the right words "—less than that."

Brett didn't know what to say. It wasn't his MO to throw someone under a bus, even in a situation like this one. "I mean, I do try, yes, and I don't know how she—"

"Listen, I'm going to shoot straight with you. I don't have the luxury of using common sense in this kind of situation. I know what probably happened. But what I have to do is use some kind of punishment here. I'm not putting this on your transcript. What I've decided to do is to give you three days' suspension. I know it's a tough pill to swallow, but it's the best I can do, given the situation."

It was better than he'd expected, at least.

"I don't know what to say. Thank you, I guess, I—"

"You don't *say* anything. What I need you to do is to go home now, and not mention this to any of your friends. If this gets back to me, it's going on your transcript, and that's that. Do you understand?"

Brett nodded, resisting the urge to smile goofily. The headmaster replaced his glasses and indicated that he should leave.

Brett left the office just as the bell was ringing for the end of the period. He walked determinedly to one of the back stairwells. Once there, he opened a door to see Michelle sitting on one of the steps. She stood up and smiled at him.

"Hey!" She said, giving him a swift kiss on the cheek.

*What the hell?*

"Hey, Miche."

"Oh, no," she said, her face dropping as she looked at Brett. "What happened with the NSL stuff?"

I listened as Brett told her everything that had happened. Watched her face as she heard what her friend had done. Somewhere within me, I could recall a time when she would have defended me, tried to explain how I "wasn't so bad." But not today.

Today she was mad. She was rolling her eyes, and Brett was telling her to calm down, not to worry about it. She was saying how awful I was.

She was supporting Brett.

The bizarreness of Michelle and Brett having a thing together was just sinking in as the ground left me again.

# CHAPTER NINE

When my eyes opened again, I was on the floor of the boardroom. I stood quickly, my legs still sore from their lack of real use. I stepped easily out of Brett's too-big shoes and sank into a chair.

I looked at Anna, who was standing in the same place she'd been before it had all happened.

"Anna, that is freakin' enough, what is going *on?*" I looked at the unmoving people in front of me. "And why are they acting like I'm not here? Seriously."

"They can't hear you, Bridget."

I threw up my hands and braced myself for another vague explanation. "Why not?"

She took a step toward me before saying quietly, "It's not the time."

There it was. Vague.

I was starting to feel frantic. "You *said* that already! What does that mean, Anna?" She said nothing. "I mean, I don't even *know* you, and here you are doing... whatever this is. It's like an intervention or something except it's...not. Plus, I don't have a problem that needs...intervention-ing."

I waited for her to speak. When she didn't, I let out a noise of exasperation. "Can you at least answer *one* question for me?"

Anna smiled. "I can try."

I sat up in the chair. "Am I dead?"

The smile faded from Anna's face, and my heart plunged. But then she shook her head.

"No, Bridget, you're not dead."

Something about the way she said it made it seem like I needed to ask my next question.

"Am I...alive?" I asked hesitantly, certain I didn't want to hear the answer.

"Not exactly."

I stared at her. She was looking sympathetically at me. I cast a fleeting glance toward the other people in the room.

"Well, *is* it a dream, or something?" I laughed nervously, worried about what this meant.

"You don't need to worry, Bridget. Not yet, anyway." She took my hand, and the smallest inkling of serenity washed over me. "All right?"

I nodded, realizing that I had no option but to be all right with that. "What did you feel, seeing what you did?"

I scoffed defensively. "Um. I don't know, I was there the first time, I don't see why I needed to see it again." That wasn't completely true. It was a little humbling to see what Brett thought about me. But, I mean, it was just *Brett*. "So are we finished now? Can I go back to school?"

Anna simply looked at me. Yeah, I knew we weren't finished yet.

"Fine," I said.

Anna glanced at the ground again, and I saw a pair of slightly worn, long, leather men's shoes.

Already I knew the drill. I stepped into them, sighing and privately shuddering to think what embarrassment I was going to have to watch next.

When the ground reappeared again, I was in my Tech Ed classroom. I knew exactly whose head I was in—Mr. Ezhno's. I watched his hands nervously organizing and reorganizing the papers on the desk. The clock on the wall told me that it was about ten minutes before anyone should be arriving. He turned to the chalkboard and opened a brand-new box of chalk. I felt him smile and realized that he was excited.

He wrote *Mr. Ezhno* on the chalkboard, considered it for a moment, and then erased it. Picking up the piece of chalk again, he wrote *John Ezhno.* He thought that might make him seem more approachable and less patronizing.

I remembered the day now. It was the first day of this school year, and Mr. Ezhno's first year teaching at our school. Judging by his thoughts now, it seemed like it was his first year teaching *ever.*

He looked at the clock again. Two minutes had passed. I remembered what happened next.

The door opened and I waltzed in, carrying a small gift box. I smiled, and walked over to his desk with my free hand out.

"Hi, my name is Bridget Duke. I thought I'd come introduce myself, since you're going to be my teacher."

I felt Mr. Ezhno's spirits rise as he shook my hand. His thoughts said something about it being *already not as bad as everyone said it would be here.*

"John Ezhno. It's nice to meet you, Bridget."

I watched myself hold out the box. It contained a

Mont Blanc pen. Meredith had sent me to class with it, in an effort to welcome the new teacher. Since it was such a small school, it was kind of a big thing when we got a new teacher. And, typically for her, Meredith was irritatingly on top of this kind of thing. I had agreed to take the gift with me, saying grudgingly that at the very least it might get me a better grade.

Mr. Ezhno opened it and was genuinely pleased by it.

"Miss Duke, I'm not sure what to say, this is so generous of you. Tell me, are you interested in Technology Education at all?"

I remembered rolling my eyes internally at the question, but having just enough decorum to keep that to myself.

"You know, I'm more into…other things. But that doesn't mean I won't enjoy your class, right?" I watched myself smile, fully aware of which smile it was. It was the suck-up smile. But Mr. Ezhno seemed to buy it fully, which made the current me feel guilty.

He laughed and agreed, saying that he, too, hoped the class would keep me interested. "Thanks again for the pen, that's really so kind of you."

"No problem, Mr. Enzo."

"It's 'Ezhno.'" He smiled, hoping to come off the right way. I knew that he hadn't.

I watched my smile ebb a bit as I said, "Okay" and then ducked out of the classroom, promising to be back soon.

Mr. Ezhno toyed with the pen as he sat there, feeling content. He thought about all of his friends, the naysayers, and felt fully behind what he'd said before. He'd said that children and teenagers weren't all bad, and that they just needed the right kind of teacher. He'd told his friends how he hoped to change his one tiny place in the world for the better, simply by teaching kids the way they needed to be taught.

Images of enthusiastic students being impressed by his technological prowess danced in his head. He was thinking of field trips and heated debates about why things worked the way they did. Awed faces of excited students, hoping that maybe *today* would be the day that he showed them one of his "Electricks," as he would call his feats of electric magic.

Still thinking optimistic thoughts, he busied himself around the classroom, trying to make it seem inviting and fun. The blocks he had set up on the front table in a Jenga shape—he'd had to get there an hour early to do it—waiting for students to choose a block to write their name on with a wood-burning pen. He thought it a clever way to remember their names and to have as a first project.

When the students started pouring into the room, a rush of nervousness went through him. He felt like he was about to step out onto a stage. He was organizing his papers once more when he heard a crashing sound come from his right. A couple of male students were laughing loudly at the pile of blocks one of them had knocked over with his backpack. They headed toward the back of the classroom, not cleaning up the mess except to kick the ones on the floor out of their path.

"That's all right, gentleman," Mr. Ezhno said, mostly to himself. He hurried over to the mess and started trying to reassemble them quickly. But every time he placed one back on the table, another one fell off. He thought regretfully of arriving an hour early simply to put his creation in the way of the door.

Once everyone was in the classroom, except for me—I knew myself to be outside waiting to come in a minute or so late—Mr. Ezhno cleared his throat and started to speak.

"Hi, everyone, uh, I'm John. John Ezhno, and I'm here to teach you about technology." He smiled jovially, but quickly realized that only a few of the students were even looking at him. He coughed again. "Could I—could I have your attention, please?" He felt guilty, like that by gaining order in his class he would somehow look like a jerk.

Just as the muttering was ceasing and more people were giving Mr. Ezhno their attention, I pulled open the door and sat down next to the seat Jillian had saved for me.

"Even hotter than last year, Duke!" Matt Churchill's voice came from the back of the classroom.

"And you're even more aggravating," I said, though I was surprised to see that enjoyment of the flattery showed all over my face, exposing the fact that I wasn't annoyed at all.

"I'd like to go ahead and get going here, so I'm going to ask you all a couple of questions. Who here thinks they might want to do something in this field when you grow up?"

"When we 'grow up'? What are we, six?" Logan said, his tone nasty. Even I had thought that was rude. Now it seemed downright disrespectful.

I felt Mr. Ezhno's embarrassment. He felt the way adults do around children when they've never had any and it's clear why.

"I still wonder what I'll be doing when I grow up,"

Mr. Ezhno said with a smile. "No, but what I meant was, do any of you intend to go into a field like this as a career?"

The silence that followed was even worse than a comment from the boys in the back.

I remembered that the rest of the class carried on that way. No one was very interested in what Mr. Ezhno said, and no one paid any attention to his instructions. When he told everyone to grab a block and began demonstrating how they were to carve their names, everyone just talked amongst themselves. I watched as I engaged in catty conversation with Jillian.

An overall feeling of unease crept upon me as I watched Mr. Ezhno pull out his completed wood block. It was impressive, and had obviously had a lot of care put into it. No one even looked up. He headed for his desk, where he spent the remainder of the class.

The world spun fast again, and I found myself in the staff lounge.

I looked down at the lunch Mr. Ezhno had packed for himself. A peanut-butter-and-honey sandwich, evidently a favorite from his childhood (and mine), a somewhat bruised banana, a thermos of clumped fettuccine alfredo left over from the restaurant he'd been to the night before and an iced tea.

He was just about to take a bite of his sandwich when he heard his name on the PA system.

*"John Ezhno, please report to the main office, John Ezhno, please report to the main office."*

He sighed and repackaged his lunch in the brown paper bag he'd just removed it from so carefully. Stuffing it back in his valise, he headed toward the office.

When he got there he was faced with what were apparently the same agog faces that he'd been noticing for days. There had been whispers and pointed looks in his direction. Now that even the receptionists were looking at him like that, he was certain something was wrong.

I spotted one of the receptionists' one-a-day calendars. This was the day of my accident.

"You called me?" Mr. Ezhno asked.

She nodded with a distinct look of disapproval and pointed toward the headmaster's office.

Puzzled, Mr. Ezhno walked in to see the headmaster looking just as disapprovingly at him from behind his desk. He shut the door.

"Kevin, what's going on?"

"Why don't you take a seat, John?"

A nervous tremor coursed through Mr. Ezhno's chest as he sat obediently on the comfortable leather couch against one wall. “Thanks,” he said, knowing it was the wrong response but having no idea what the right response could be. He knew he hadn’t done anything wrong, but that didn’t mean he couldn’t be afraid.

“Do you have any idea why I’ve called you in here today, John?”

Mr. Ezhno’s apprehension rose slightly as he recognized the fact that he was being spoken to like a badly behaved student.

“No, I don’t.”

“Something to do with Meredith Duke?”

Mr. Ezhno’s eyebrows came together in sincere puzzlement at the mention of my stepmother’s name.

I, too, had no idea what this was about.

“All right, John, I’m going to be honest with you. I haven’t known you long and don’t know much about your character. So, unfortunately, I have to go by what the students have been talking about. Rumor has it you’re…involved with Mrs. Duke.”

I felt the combined—and substantial—shock of Mr. Ezhno and myself.

*What* rumor? Who had started *that* one?

“Excuse me?” Mr. Ezhno sputtered.

“Miss Duke came in here complaining that she had trouble getting to your class on time, yada yada yada, and then by the end of the conversation told me about how the 'real problem'—" he put the words in finger quotes "—was coming from home."

The headmaster sounded tired as he rehashed our meeting. "She said that she's been uncomfortable with her stepmother's new…suitor, and that she has to see him five days a week. She also said that she was tired of the meetings that were happening between you and Mrs. Duke."

"The *meetings* she's tired of are parent-teacher conferences. And of course she's tired of them—they're measures of behavioral correction. Hell, *I'm* tired of them. Mrs. Duke is a perfectly nice woman, but there's absolutely nothing between us at those meetings except talk about Bridget's behavior in school, I assure you."

I felt the anger he felt toward me. He thought that I'd made up this huge lie to get out of trouble for tardiness. I understood that. If I'd been scared and creative enough, maybe I *would* have woven a web like this.

"Well, the problem has come to be this, John. It seems she's let this romance between the two of you—whether it be fictional or no—" he looked skeptical "—slip to the rest of the school."

Mr. Ezhno's heart was racing. "So that's what all the looks I've been getting are about?"

"Probably. I waited a few days, you know, to see if things would die down, but the rumors are all over the place. You must see the problem I'm faced with here, surely."

The headmaster waited, and I felt irritated with him for being so condescending.

"Well, of course, that can't happen, I realize that. But what do you expect me to do?"

"John, I'm not able to keep on a staff member if he or she has become involved with a student's parent. Especially when it hasn't been kept quiet, and it's such a small school as this. Even more especially when it's a high-profile student. And let's face it, you haven't been here long, you don't have any tenure or reputation to speak of. Maybe things would be different if you'd been here longer."

"But I *haven't* been having an affair, I hardly know the woman!" Panic rose. "I realize how it must look, but you can't do this to…me…you can't just…"

"Look, I know how frustrating this must be, John…"

Mr. Ezhno thought about his words carefully before speaking, so that they didn't come off as "nuh-uh!"

"Listen, Ransic, this isn't ethical and you know it. You know Bridget Duke, and you must see that this is an act for attention, or something else. I just can't believe you'd fire me because of the lie of a contemptible little girl like that."

The headmaster looked like he was concentrating as he stared down at the pen he was fiddling with. He set it down.

"John. My hands are tied. I've had parents call in already, worried about how this is affecting students and equality in the classroom. With Bridget's father being, well, who he is....do you know who her father is?"

"Yeah, I watch ESPN," Mr. Ezhno spat, thinking irritatedly of the expensive sports package he'd just bought for his brand-new TV.

"So then you know that he's powerful."

A horrible thought slipped into Mr. Ezhno's mind. "Donates a lot of money to the school, does he?"

A minuscule hesitation gave Mr. Ezhno the validation he'd feared.

"John, he's going to be furious when and if he finds out about this. And beyond the Duke family, the *school's* reputation is at stake here. This is a prestigious institution, and this kind of unprofessionalism just will not fly." He looked earnestly at Mr. Ezhno. "I know that there's a chance this isn't the case, but I have no way of *really* knowing that. It might have been different if no one else knew, maybe there would have been time for a meeting or something like that. But the problem is that, at this point, it's common knowledge even if it is a fabrication."

Mr. Ezhno's heart was still racing. Only now he was feeling something I'd felt before, too. The feeling that the pin had been pulled on a grenade and nothing could be done to stop it from exploding.

Just as Mr. Ezhno was standing to leave and his thoughts turned toward resentment of me, I felt the rush of leaving his mind.

"How did that *happen?*" I asked Anna, as soon as I could see again. I now felt my own frenzy as strongly as I'd felt Mr. Ezhno's. "I never said he was, like, *doing* stuff with her!" I concentrated and things began to come back to me. "I said some things that…I guess they could have sounded that way…" I thought of my poorly chosen words. Like how I'd said I had to see him five days a week.

I winced as I remembered my conversation with the headmaster. Now that I thought of it, I'd had no clear segue between talking about Meredith's imaginary lover and talking about how much I hated the parent-teacher conferences.

I looked at Anna, who was still watching me with that same blandly compassionate look on her face.

It was like she knew what I was thinking.

"But I didn't mean to do any of that," I insisted. "I just wanted to…get out of the office…" I heard my weak words, which so obviously didn't pass as an excuse. "But I didn't say anything to anyone else, I'm completely sure of that."

I was glad to say this honestly. I thought carefully and decided that I truly hadn't said anything to that effect.

The expression on Anna's face, however, said otherwise.

"I think things will become clearer after our next journey," she said lightly.

I nodded, unable to do much else, and looked down the floor.

Now it was time to squeeze into the Carfagni Mary Jane shoes I'd admired for so long.

## CHAPTER TEN

I found myself in the girls' bathroom at school, looking into a mirror at Michelle's reflection. Her eyes were watery and red. Her face was the same color, with a tinge of purple to it. I watched her adjust herself, wiping away the mascara that had run beneath her eyes.

After looking around to be sure she was the only one in the bathroom, Michelle turned to the side with one hand on her stomach and stood up as straight as possible. I was surprised to see how narrow she was, but even more surprised by her thoughts, which said otherwise. She looked critically at her lower stomach, which came out a fraction of an inch more than the rest of her toned tummy.

"Gawd," she muttered to herself. I watched

incredulously as she found pretend flaw after pretend flaw on her body. *My torso's too thick,* she thought, trying to suck in the portion beneath her ribs. She looked concave.

And she had a thought that stunned me.

*I know that if I lose any more weight I'll look too thin, but maybe I want to look too thin.*

I yearned to be able to communicate with her, to tell her how stupid that was, and that "too thin" wasn't a good thing, that it was more of an insult than anything else, but I was powerless.

The bell rang, and she hurried to put a breath mint in her mouth. Taking a second to give herself a final, critical once-over in the mirror, she left the bathroom. She felt embarrassed to be walking the halls. She felt like everyone was going to see her for what she was, whatever that might be. There was a word Michelle was avoiding in the back of her mind. One she couldn't seem to bring herself to say or admit.

She walked into the women's locker room and headed toward the locker I'd made her choose next to mine.

"*There* you are, God, since when are you late? You're probably just late because I need to talk to you. Judging by *my* luck." I watched myself complain, chewing on the Bubblicious gum from my purse.

Michelle sighed as she asked, "Why, what's up?"

I took off my earrings as I launched into my story about how completely unfair it was that Mr. Ezhno was even allowed to teach. I complained that he obviously hated kids anyway, so why was he even teaching?

I thought self-consciously of the optimism he'd felt on his first day and felt sad.

But the Bridget in the locker room carried on with her bitching.

"I was *seriously* only thirty seconds late. And it wasn't even my fault! It was his be*loved* Meredith's fault." I could feel that Michelle knew, just as I did, that I'd been later than just thirty seconds. Michelle formed a response in her head. One where she asked how it could have possibly been Meredith's fault. Ultimately, she changed her mind and went with the easy answer that wouldn't start an argument.

I got the feeling that this happened often.

"Yeah, that sucks." Michelle started to pull on her shorts, looking at her thighs. To me they looked so thin they were on the verge of cowboy legs, but she seemed to see sausages. She pulled them up to her hips, and felt self-conscious of her hips, which she was convinced were spilling over the waistband. *They aren't,* I tried desperately to tell her from my impotent place inside her mind. That's just what it looks like when something's not the right size! Feet don't fit into shoes that are too small, for example—I thought of the Mary Janes—and that's just because they're not the right size. But the only thing Michelle heard from me was my thoughtless observation.

"You know, you should really buy new shorts this year. Those are getting a little tight on your hips."

I cringed and wished I could take it back. It came off as insulting, which I really hadn't meant it to be.

Michelle looked at me and watched with envy as I pulled on my waistband, which was huge on me.

"Mine, on the other hand..." I said, like it was a huge burden. I thought wearily of how many times I'd acted like a good thing was tiresome. Like in mandatory chorus class in middle school, where I'd said I couldn't sing from my stomach because my abs were too tight. And when I said that I couldn't wear some pairs of sunglasses because my eyelashes pressed against the lenses from being so long.

I was surprised that Michelle didn't seem angry with me. In fact, her only thought was that she was jealous. She didn't want to have to think about her waistband anymore.

"Okay, so what happened when you came in late?"

she asked, and then went back to trying to stretch out the pants so that she could still get away with wearing size small. When she wore a small, it meant she was a small, dammit. If she moved up to a medium, it would mean she wasn't small anymore.

It would mean she'd gotten bigger.

The other me, oblivious to the thoughts in Michelle's head, continued bitching.

"Basically, he sent me to the office with this totally stupid note talking about how I'm some kind of menace. Oh! And he said something about me distracting other students who were *trying to pay attention*. It was so stupid. So then I had to wait for, like, *ever,* with three of Winchester Prep's Least Wanted. Are you even listening, Michelle? Or are you just going to rip your pants trying to make them fit?" Michelle had hardly been getting stressed out about my story, but thought she'd heard everything I'd said.

"Oh, sorry, go on. I was listening."

Michelle watched, feeling ashamed, as I sighed and looked condescendingly at her.

"So, finally I go in, right, and then I'm about to be super nice and just say something about how I promise not to be late anymore, and how homework's been hard lately, and then Mr. Ezhno actually *called* the office…" I carried on.

"Seriously?" Michelle gave out the generic response, hoping it would satisfy me.

Apparently it did.

"Seriously. So I knew I was going to have to think fast, and really all I wanted to do was to get out of there, right? So I start talking about how Meredith's always got this 'male guest' over."

Michelle stared fixedly at her waistband in an effort to not look surprised by what I was saying. She thought quickly, trying to remember if I'd ever said anything about a male guest before.

But I carried on.

"I just complained about how she and Mr. Ezhno were always meeting and stuff, and how he was like in *love* with her, and how everything he does is because of that. And how they're totally doing it."

"Wait, what?" Michelle asked. She'd been paying attention, but was worried that this situation was something she was supposed to already know all about.

The whistle blew, and I rolled my eyes.

Michelle spent the rest of the class trying to ask me what I'd meant back there in the locker room, without revealing that she may not have been listening very well.

As soon as gym class ended and Michelle no longer had to hear me complain about Meredith, she dashed off to find Jillian. When she finally found her, she pulled her out the side doors of the school, saying it was an emergency and they needed to talk.

Jillian's eyebrows wrinkled with concern as she told Michelle to spit it out; her heart couldn't take the suspense.

"Jill, do you ever remember Bridget talking about something going on between Mr. Ezhno and her stepmom?"

Jillian's eyes widened, "No! What are you talking about?"

Jillian tugged on Michelle's arm to sit down at one of the picnic tables dedicated to the graduating class of 1989.

Michelle looked around to be sure no one was listening.

"Well, I'm not really sure *what* I'm talking about. We were in gym class, and she was complaining about Mr. Ezhno—that's his name, right, your Tech Ed teacher?"

"Yeah, go on," Jillian responded, looking eager.

"Okay, so she's talking about how he sent her out of the classroom today, and about how she was sent to see the headmaster and everything. And I'm not really sure how she got from one point to the other, but somehow she started talking about how she told Ransic about the affair Meredith's been having with Mr. Ezhno."

"Omigod," Jillian said, her fingertips over her mouth.

"Right? So then, I didn't really want to ask her what she was talking about, so I just acted like what she said didn't surprise me, or whatever. She said stuff about how he's in love with her stepmom, and like that's why he acts how he does."

Jillian was nodding her head as she followed the story. Michelle kept going, surprised that Jillian didn't know anything either.

"So then, I'm listening to it all, trying to think of an explanation for what she's saying or trying to think of how I must be misunderstanding her, when she says this—are you ready?"

Jillian looked like she was about to explode.

"She said that Meredith and Mr. Ezhno are 'totally doing it,'" Michelle quoted. I watched Jillian's face.

"So then that's it? Well, then, no buts about it, I guess, she's totally confirmed it. That is *so weird*."

I couldn't believe what I was hearing. Between what I had told Ransic myself, what I had also told Michelle and then what I had confirmed to Jillian the next day, I'd gotten someone fired and destroyed my own reputation.

It really was *all* my fault.

"But we can't say anything," Michelle said quickly.

"No, definitely not. But maybe I should ask her if what she said to you was true," Jillian said, thoughtfully.

"Oh, I don't know...can you ask her without it looking like I wasn't listening? I really don't need her mad at me right now." She rolled her eyes.

"Definitely, don't even worry about it. We're all friends, I'll just say you told me what she said and then I'll ask her if it's true."

Michelle hesitated before agreeing that it was probably the best way. Then, just as I expected might happen next, the ground went away and I found myself in my own dining room.

Jillian was eating a banana and reading the nutritional facts on the side of the cereal box, and Michelle was watching me eat a bowl of the cereal. I could feel her longing to have some, but resisting. I caught Michelle's gaze and looked at her.

"Michelle, eat something." I said it not like a concerned friend, but like a dictator.

Michelle noticed that, too.

"I'm not hungry, it's fine," she responded, speaking loudly over her stomach, which had chosen that inconvenient time to rumble. Michelle figured I wouldn't hear it, that I'd be busy focusing on what I would say next.

As usual.

I hated that it was true.

"Michelle."

"Seriously, Bridget."

"What, do you not *like* what I have to eat or something?"

"I'm just not hungry, okay?"

As I looked at my ringing phone, thoughts of a conversation she'd had with Brett were floating through her mind. She was mad at me. Upset by what I'd done to Brett. Brett, who was secretly her *boyfriend*. Secret because she knew I'd mercilessly make fun of her if I knew. She knew I wouldn't simply let her be happy. I would only give her crap for it.

I tried to wrap my mind around that concept.

"Fine. As long as you're not just overreacting to Jillian's little health freak-out over there. It's not like she even knows what she's talking about."

Michelle was trying to come up with a good excuse for why she wasn't eating, and trying not to shout at me for always making fun of people, when Meredith came in the room. I was surprised by the admiration Michelle felt looking at her. She gazed longingly at Meredith's well-put-together outfit, which hung on her slender frame. I could feel Michelle yearn to look as beautiful as my stepmother.

"Oh, good morning, girls!"

I noticed, as Michelle did, that though Meredith had just put on lipstick, there was not even a tiny smudge on her teeth. Another small twinge of admiration.

"I'm having a party tonight."

"Are you?"

"Yes. I thought your flight wasn't until four. Are you leaving *now?*"

"Oh, well, I'm meeting up with somebody beforehand and I'll have about an hour and a half before the shuttle picks me up after that. I just want to be ready to go in case the meeting runs long."

"Meeting with who?"

Michelle looked at me, suddenly worried what the answer would be.

*"Who?"* I asked again.

"John Ezhno." Michelle looked at Jillian, who had paused halfway through chewing a bite of her banana.

*"Really."* Man, I sounded nasty.

"Yes, does that surprise you?"

Michelle and Jillian both looked at the tennis match-style argument that was ensuing. I felt the small shock that Michelle was feeling. Shock that Meredith was flaunting her romance so brashly.

"Um, yes, does *that* surprise *you?*"

"Bridget, stop it."

"*You* stop it."

"Bridget, I mean it! You know, I wouldn't have to keep seeing him if you or your father would just—"

Michelle had the uncomfortable feeling she'd felt so many times at my house. She hated being an innocent bystander stuck in the room with an argument, and, with the way I often acted toward people, it wasn't unusual to find oneself in that situation.

Michelle looked resolutely at her lap, ignoring the scene around her. It felt like she shouldn't be there. She looked at Jillian, who was watching Meredith leave the room.

Michelle and Jillian both looked at me, and I was surprised to see that my face had turned red.

"Wha...?" I said around my mouthful of cereal.

They both tried to act like nothing had happened all the way up until Jillian's phone rang and she had to leave. Then she winked at Michelle.

Jillian gathered up her things, and I heard myself close the door on her. Michelle was sitting by herself on the soft leather sofa set in my living room.

She was thinking of how to talk to me.

She was trying to decide whether to admit something to me, confront me about something or tell me a secret of hers, but I couldn't tell what any of them were. Her thoughts were fleeting, going by way too fast.

When I slumped down onto the couch and turned on the TV, the feat of trying to have a real conversation with me seemed even harder to Michelle. I felt guilty for being so unapproachable.

"Bridget? Can we talk for a second?"

"Sure."

Michelle's heart beat a little faster as adrenaline rose in her chest. "Like, without the TV on?" She watched me sigh as if it was a huge burden to listen to anything she had to say.

"It's kind of...embarrassing to talk about. I just

think…that you kind of…make me feel bad about myself sometimes." Michelle spoke quickly, hoping that I wouldn't just instantly act like a bitch. Maybe I'd at least take a *moment* to be compassionate. We were supposed to be friends, after all. Michelle's hope evaporated when she heard me scoff.

"I what?"

"It's just…I'm sensitive about my weight and—"

"Oh, shut *up,* Michelle."

I felt the adrenaline in Michelle escalate again. How *dare* Bridget respond with that?

Michelle looked at me. She was thinking of Brett, the conversation about the gym shorts, Outdoor Ed, the many casually offensive comments I'd cast off without thinking.

"No, Bridget, I won't shut up! You say things all the time that make me feel really bad about myself, and it's just not okay!"

Michelle wondered for a moment if she should just spit out the truth. But would she be saying it just for the shock factor, or because she actually thought I might change my behavior?

"Like what!" I spewed.

"Oh, my God, Bridget, you really don't know?" Michelle shouted with disbelief. How could any person be so unaware of what she'd said so many times?

"No, I *really don't know.* Are you seriously telling me that *you* feel fat?"

"Yes!" She burst out the answer, trying to hold in the truth.

"Oh, puh-*leeze.* You're deluded. You're crazy! And I'm not going to listen to crazy talk." I watched myself look Michelle up and down, my lip curled. "*I* didn't say you're fat, Michelle. I *wouldn't* say anything like that—"

There was a difference between *I didn't say you were fat* and *I don't think you're fat*—it was clear now.

"—but if you *feel* fat, eat a salad or something, I don't know. It's all in your head. Just don't blame *your* insecurities on me!"

Tears started to well in Michelle's eyes, but she blinked them away. Of all people to break down in front of, Bridget was certainly not one of them, Michelle thought. She thought about my words. What if it was all in her head? What if I really hadn't said anything too bad, and it was just her imagination?

*No,* she thought stubbornly, *it's not all in my head.*

"It's not *my* insecurities only, Bridget, you're always making comments about what I should do to look prettier and telling me my clothes are all wrong, and I just can't—"

"I'm your friend, Michelle, it's called advice?" I paused at my realization. "Michelle, is this about the gym shorts? They're from *freshman year.* And they just don't fit you anymore!"

She had no response. Bridget just wasn't going to understand. She was glad she hadn't told me the whole truth.

I think I knew it now.

TIME SPED BY LIKE fast-forwarding through a movie. I could hardly see any of the scenes that passed me. When the reel slowed down enough for me to actually pay attention, I was still in Michelle's head, staring at the ornate front door of my house and standing next to Jillian, who had just rung the doorbell.

I heard my distant voice call from upstairs for them to come in.

"Are you sure you feel up to this?" Jillian asked Michelle, who nodded, feeling friendly affection toward her one—real, she thought—best friend.

They came up the stairs and found me observing the clothes in my closet.

"Hey. Do you need help bringing in the rest of the beer? Jillian, why don't you help her?"

Michelle stopped dead. I felt the alarm she was feeling as she realized her mistake, and her worry as she imagined what I might say or do next, how I might explode at her.

"The *rest* of the beer?" she asked quietly, and watched as I turned to Jillian.

"Tell me there's a 'rest of the beer.'"

Michelle felt her fear turn into anger as she watched me use one of my favorite bitch techniques: the laugh, and the shake of the head.

"What the hell is *wrong* with you, Michelle? God, it's like you're stupid or something. One minute you're telling me you're all insecure about *everything* and the next minute you're ruining my party. Great job. Seriously."

As had always been her flaw when it came to getting mad, Michelle felt the inescapable urge to cry. A memory resurfaced in her mind of the anger and embarrassment she'd felt after the prank I'd taken the rap for at Outdoor Ed.

"But Bridget, you just said to get some beer, you didn't say—"

She started to explain that she didn't know she was responsible for the whole party, and that her brother only bought what he *did* buy because he thought it was for just the three girls. It had been hard enough to convince him to do even that.

"I gave you Meredith's credit card and told you to get beer for the party, how is it *not* obvious that you're going to need more? If you really didn't know, then why didn't you just *call* me and ask how much?"

"I tried! You didn't pick up!" It was true, Michelle thought, she had tried to call. She wasn't calling to ask how much she needed, though, she was just calling to say that all she could get was just the two six-packs. She'd known it would go over badly.

"Bullshit."

Michelle could tell this conversation would go nowhere, and that the easiest thing was to just apologize.

"I'm sorry, it was stupid—"

"You're right, so why are you still here?"

Michelle's heart jolted for a moment. *This is how it always is with Bridget,* she thought. Since Michelle didn't want to be on my bad side, she'd had to swallow all kinds of pride to stay friends—even if she hated it.

"What do you mean?" she asked, afraid of what Bridget—I—might say.

"I *mean* why aren't you driving back to get your brother to go buy more?"

Michelle took a second to breathe normally again, before she came upon the second hurdle.

"Um. Well, he's not at home."

"I'm sorry, *what?* Your brother has been sitting in that stupid gaming chair since we were like, six. What do you mean he's not home?" I felt Michelle's pang of defensiveness for her brother.

"He went out with a friend."

"*God,* Michelle. Now what the hell are we going to do?"

TIME SPED BY AGAIN, and I found that Michelle was standing in my kitchen. She was eating the chips and salsa Liam had brought to the party, and something in her mind said that she was doing something wrong. I worried about what it might be, wondering if she was getting back at me in some way. She spotted the box of Oreos and took out four of the cookies, then put one back.

*Three,* she thought to herself, *three is okay.*

"Having your own private eating contest, Miche?"

She turned to see me stumbling past with a drink in one hand, and my arm around Matt Churchill.

She instantly felt embarrassed, and so did the current me. I'd said it *only* because there was an impromptu hot dog-eating contest being held on the back deck. But as soon as I heard the words come out of my mouth, I knew it was the wrong thing to say. Michelle obviously didn't know what I was referencing.

I watched myself go stumbling off, still laughing. Michelle was right, I said that kind of thing to her all the time. I said things that sounded okay in my head but that just weren't.

The doorbell rang, and I heard myself shout "Pizza!" to the crowd. I ran by in my black bikini.

I could feel Michelle's envy at my confidence, at my ability to wander around unselfconsciously in a tiny bathing suit like that one.

What she didn't notice was how much bonier she was than me.

And she had no idea how all that self-assurance she noticed in me would go straight down the drain after I opened the door.

Michelle walked upstairs, hoping no one would see her go. As she entered my room, I could feel her guilt combining with embarrassment. I couldn't figure out what her problem was. She was acting like she'd hidden a body in the backyard or something.

She opened the door to my bathroom and closed it behind her. She tried to lock the door for a few seconds before remembering that I had said it was broken.

She felt dread. She hoped no one would come in.

Michelle looked at her reflection in the mirror, and her frame of mind grew worse still. She stared at her stomach, seeming to believe that the chips and salsa she'd eaten downstairs had made her abdomen expand offensively. She started to cry, feeling like she was doing so *far* too often, and lifted up the toilet seat.

Suddenly guessing what was coming, I still felt stunned as she knelt down in front of the toilet and stuck her fingers down her throat until she heaved.

Michelle threw up again and again, her face throbbing with the blood that was rushing to it. She leaned back on her feet, feeling something I'd been feeling a lot recently.

Disgusted with her own behavior.

She wished she wasn't this way, and wished she could take it back. But then she realized that what she wanted to take back was the junk food she'd been eating. She vowed never to do it again. But she knew it was an empty promise to herself.

She was just vomiting again when the door opened.

A shriek escaped Michelle's mouth as she saw my shocked face leave the doorway again.

# CHAPTER ELEVEN

I stared at Michelle, who was still flipping mutely through her notepad on the conference table.

I didn't know what to say, or what to think. How does someone go about apologizing for contributing to something so dangerous?

Until now, I'd had no idea that Michelle was bulimic. Though suddenly it seemed so obvious.

Certainly, I thought, I would have been more careful about what I said to her if I had known. If I'd had any idea. But a small voice in my head asked a question: Why weren't you careful what you said to her just because she's your friend?

And for that, I had no response.

I turned to Anna. "I didn't know."

"Of course you didn't." She said it sincerely. Not sarcastically, like I always meant that phrase. "Do you need to take a moment, or shall we continue on?"

I glanced at Michelle, longing to talk to her and have her hear me. But I knew that it was impossible.

Why was she even friends with me? Sure, after the Kotex event, I'd sworn to her it wasn't me, and told her the truth—that I'd been trying to undo what they'd done. I knew there had been a brief period in the beginning of high school when I was a good and normal friend, but now…even I could see that I was toxic for her.

"Let's go," I said, standing up. Anna pointed down to a pair of dark-brown Steve Madden loafers on the ground.

My gut lurched.

"No, stop." I stepped away from the shoes.

Anna looked at me. I shook my head.

"I can't go into Liam's mind, I know how I was. I was wrong, and I know it." I stepped toward her. "Please, can't we just…skip him, or something? I can't *know* for sure what he thinks of me. It'll hurt too much."

I knew that my plea wouldn't get me anywhere.

Anna smiled composedly.

"We have to. I'm sorry."

I found myself on the blacktop at my elementary school, walking toward the playground, which was about a hundred yards away. I shuddered as I guessed what day it was.

Liam looked down at his feet, and I noticed that he was wearing his *Jetsons* T-shirt.

He climbed up the slide and headed toward the red tunnel I used to hide in as a kid after such traumas as being the last called for Red Rover. Sure enough, there I was, my face covered in smushed bananas and streaked with tears.

"Hi, Bridget," Liam said, his voice husky even then.

"Hi," I said, the word coming out more like a question as I launched into a new set of tears.

"Oh, don't cry!" He crawled toward me a little bit. He placed an awkward little eight-year-old hand on my shoulder and patted.

"But I'm…so…embarrassed!" I said, my breath catching on every word.

"I know. But it's okay, they'll forget about it soon enough." He thought desperately for something comforting to say. "If it helps, they didn't tell anyone else what they were going to do. I think it just happened."

"I don't…even…like…bananas!" I said, still more desperately.

"I know. But hey, at least you know that if there *had* been a banana-eating-contest, you would have won it."

Little me rolled her eyes, thinking what a small consolation prize that was.

"But I can't believe that I fell for it. I mean, why did I think they were putting the blindfold on me?"

Liam continued to pat my shoulder comfortingly, imitating the adults he'd seen do the same thing in upsetting situations. I was impressed to find that Liam didn't seem to be holding back any laughter. He seemed to think it was just as unfair as I did.

"I have a deck of cards in my cubby. Do you want to play with me?"

I nodded, touched by his willingness to leave recess to play with me. It was, after all, the ultimate sacrifice.

Liam told me to go ahead inside, he had to get something first. He watched as I skipped into the school, and then he walked resolutely toward the sponsors of the banana-eating contest.

"Hey, Tammy, Jenny, come here. I want to talk to you."

Even the current me felt intimidated watching the

girls exchange an amused look and walk toward him. They might as well have been cracking their knuckles or hitting their palms with a baseball bat.

At least he was the same height as they were. That was a luxury most boys didn't have in elementary school. He didn't feel frightened at all as they walked over to him. All he felt was contempt.

"What do you want, Wee-em?" Jenny asked, giving a loud guffaw at the nickname she'd starting using for him three years ago.

"That wasn't nice what you did to Bridget."

"Well, we weren't trying to be nice!" Tammy said, her high voice ringing in his ears.

He felt angry just looking at them. "Still, you shouldn't have done that and I think you should apologize."

The two girls laughed boisterously again, and Jenny pulled a banana from the crate on the ground. A teacher had brought the fruit to give as a treat today, since it was Friday. It was a nice idea, but, Liam considered, he should have been outside making sure this kind of thing didn't happen.

"I didn't know you wanted some, too." She flattened the banana on his face.

Liam pushed her hand away and ignored the other students who were laughing.

"You can put as many bananas as you want in our faces, Jenny, but we could never look as stupid as you do." Her mouth fell open, and Liam turned on his heel and walked casually inside, flinging the banana from his face to the ground.

Too cool for an eight-year-old.

The ground fell away as soon as he ran in the door. I didn't need to see it from Liam's perspective to remember the rest of the day. We'd played Crazy Eights for the rest of recess, and Liam had stood by my side and protected me from Jenny and Tammy for the rest of third grade.

That day should have shown me what real friends were. Instead it marked the beginning of my quest to be "in" with those girls, so they'd never, ever treat me like that again.

THE NEXT PLACE WE LANDED was my patio. I was glad to see that we hadn't ended up at the scene of the breakup.

It was clearly late into the night of my last party, and I had a feeling that I was going to come crawling around the corner any second.

Liam was talking on the phone with a voice I recognized as his mother's.

"Well, just try to drive home anyone you can. I'm disappointed that Meredith allowed drinking at one of Bridget's parties, but I suppose we have to do what we can to make sure none of them end up out on the road. You didn't have anything to drink?"

"Nah. And I don't think Meredith actually knew about the party at all," Liam said, waving his hand at the suggestion even though she couldn't see him.

"Good. Well, once again, I'm proud of you, Liam."

"Thanks, Ma." He smiled into the phone.

"How's Bridget doing?"

"Mmm," he said looking in the window for me. "I'm not sure. She was drinking kind of a lot tonight."

"I thought she didn't drink?"

"Yeah, she doesn't, which is why she's bound to be sick in the morning."

His mother chuckled. "I guess we all have to learn the hard way. Did everyone enjoy the party, do you think?"

"Yeah, I think so. I think most of 'em just came to get drunk, but none of them are being rude to her or anything."

This observation shook me. What did that mean? Did he expect them to be rude to me?

"Well, that's good. Don't worry, honey, she'll settle

down soon. She'll get back to herself one of these days, I'm sure of it."

Doubt entered his mind. "Hope so." He looked down at the brown shoes I'd just stepped into and felt another pang of some emotion I couldn't quite identify. "All right, well, you better get to bed. I think I'll drive a couple of these guys home, and then come home myself."

"Okay, drive safely, I don't want anything to happen to you. You know it's not that I don't trust *your* driving, it's—"

"—other people, I know." Liam smiled again. He'd heard her say it so many times. "'Bye, don't wait up."

"You know I will!"

He shook his head and closed his phone. And then, there I was, crawling on my hands and knees looking for Meredith's earring. Which, incidentally, I would find on my dresser in the morning. It turned out I'd never put the second one on, which meant not only that I was losing my mind, but also that I'd walked around like a pirate the whole night.

"Bridge?" Liam squinted his eyes into the darkness to see who it was. Judging by the ice-blond hair, he decided it was me.

"Yeah?" I responded after my startled squeal.

"What are you…uh, what are you doin'?" He crouched down, hoping that it wasn't something he didn't know how to handle.

"My earring?"

"Did you lose it?" Liam asked, thinking of all the times he'd looked all over the place for something I'd lost. *It's probably still in her room,* he thought. I was taken aback by his accuracy.

"I did."

"All right, let's look for it then. Do you know that it's out here somewhere?" Liam watched me nod and then try to stand. He was braced for what he was sure was going to turn into a nasty spill. Then, to only my own surprise at the time, I fell. He helped me stand.

"Liam…" I mumbled.

"Y'all right, Bridget? Why don't you sit down."

"My earring—"

"I know." He helped me to the seat he'd just vacated.

"It looks like, um…an earring that's, uh. It's like a silver, sort of loops around…"

Liam laughed at my vague description, and at the fact that I hadn't thought to simply show him the other one.

I watched his hand tuck my hair behind my ear to

look at the earring. He seemed to be sensing the familiarity that went along with this affectionate touch just as much as I had.

He looked into my eyes. I noticed, with a twinge of mortification, that I didn't look as cool and collected as I had hoped. Instead, I looked a lot like a deer in headlights.

I listened to Liam's internal battle. He cared for me, just as he had for so long. He looked at me, and saw the eight-year-old version of me with banana all over my face, and remembered my embarrassment at the pool after I'd knocked my own tooth out. More recently than that, he envisioned me the moment before we first kissed.

The moment after.

And then the genuinely distraught expression on my face as he'd ended our relationship.

I felt the devil on his shoulder—or maybe it was the angel—bring up another vision of me.

One in which I'd gone on to become friends with Tammy and Jenny, despite what they'd done to me and how long I'd hated them.

Another, in which I was telling a girl she couldn't be part of our group in social studies. Another one, where I talked enthusiastically about the flaws of every girl we knew. And another, where I told Michelle that she looked like a slut in the top she was wearing. I'd said that her boobs were too big for it—back when she'd had some—and that a person like her couldn't get away with that, but that *I* could because my chest was smaller.

And then another memory, where his friends had reported that I'd been flirting with them "hardcore" and that they all kind of felt weird about it, and thought he should know.

Wow, that was embarrassing.

The last thought that flitted through his mind was a simple one: *She just isn't the same girl she used to be.*

He furrowed his eyebrows and looked down at our hands. They looked right, in a way, to both of us, but at the same time…it seemed like that era had passed.

"I'm so tired of being like this, Liam."

Liam froze, trying hard not to misunderstand what I said for the better.

"Like what?" he asked carefully.

"It's…hard to say, I don't know. I feel like every day is this struggle to keep my life the way it's been for however long. And I think…that it's so I'm happy. But I'm not really very happy with who I am or whatever. Am I?"

He watched my forehead wrinkle as I labored for the

words. Liam thought about what I'd said, hoping that maybe this was it. Maybe I was having one of those epiphanies. His thumb moved over my cheekbone. He said nothing, not wanting to stop me from having any other realizations that might bring me back to the way I used to be.

"I'm not saying anything right. I think it was the tequila. I don't even *like* to drink!"

Liam watched as I gave an open shrug, and remembered the many times I'd done the same gesture in the past. Every time he'd let me win a race, for example, I used to put my hands up in the same way as if I was saying "Sorry, I don't know *how* I'm so fast!"

"That makes five of us. You, me, Michelle, Jillian and Anna." He said the names of my friends and Anna. I felt his hope that maybe I'd realize there were people like me.

People I didn't *have* to try to impress.

"Right. Five of us."

He stopped me from falling again, realizing that his attempt to make me feel better hadn't had the effect he'd hoped for.

"Come on, cliché drunk girl, let's get you to your bed." He weakened a bit as he heard me laugh at his joke. He could tell the difference between my well-practiced "cute" laugh and my real laugh. It was obvious which one he preferred.

As he held my body close to his own, he felt the melancholy of having to do the "right" thing by ending it all with me. I felt him push the reasons for our breakup from his mind and just feel me as I melted into him.

We got all the way up to my room, and he tried to keep his thoughts away from asking to stay overnight with me. He figured that by the time I woke up in the morning, I'd be back to my new normal again. And that wasn't something he wanted to see.

I was starting to kind of get that.

He dropped me on the bed and tucked me in, noticing the picture of us that still stood on my bedside table. It was one taken on the Fourth of July at my aunt's house a few years before. He looked around my room for a moment to see the other pictures, some of which were obviously chosen because they were good ones of me, not necessarily because they marked an occasion.

"Liam…" He felt my hand on his forearm. He always used to like it when I did that.

"Yeah, B?"

"Do you ever miss me?"

If it wasn't such a huge, sad question he might have laughed. Instead he just answered more truthfully than

I realized. "I do miss you." Every day. Every time he saw me. He missed the real me.

My grip tightened on his arm, and it felt—I knew—to both of us like it was really just us in the world for that moment. Acting impulsively, he touched my hair, remembering how soft it was. He took a second to feel weird that I was so exactly the same in some ways.

He shook himself from his reverie and stood. He pulled my shoes off, tucked me in and then walked to the door.

Liam stopped, wondering if maybe he should just stay with me for a few minutes more. He questioned if I'd even want him there. Fool, I thought. Of course I would.

"You all right, Bridget?"

He watched me nod, my eyes shut, and he took a step toward me.

But then I spoke out of nowhere. "'K. I'll see you on Monday then."

"Monday." He gave me another chance. "You'll be okay 'til then?"

"I'm fine." I heard myself lie.

I looked critically at my face, my mouth hanging unattractively slack, and my makeup gone.

But what Liam saw as he looked at me was different.

To him, I looked more like myself than I had in over a year. I wasn't trying, pretending or faking anything. And that, he thought, was beautiful.

But in his head, Liam confirmed suspicions I'd never have imagined were there. He saw me as having moved on. I'd changed, and so had my feelings for him, along with the rest of me.

I couldn't believe how wrong both of us had been about each other, again and again.

The now familiar feeling of the world leaving me came back.

# CHAPTER TWELVE

When the boardroom materialized around me, I felt numb. I reached for the chair I knew was behind me and sat.

"Why did you show me that? I didn't…ruin any lives or anything in that one." My voice sounded unlike my own. Small and shy—two things I'd never thought of myself as.

Anna sat down in her chair at the head of the table.

"You must understand that the reason we're here today is not to show you that anyone hates you."

"Well, then why *are* we here, because that's what it feels like!" I said it too loud, the way that children yell at their parents when they're more upset with themselves than anyone else.

"We're here to show you…who you are. Or at least whom you've become."

Anna looked at Liam, and then at me.

"I want you to understand how people see you, and how your actions matter," she went on. "You must learn that your place in the world is important. You've been given the power to affect people, just as we all have, and it's important—no, *vital*—that you do the right thing with it."

"Can we just go?" My tone was sharp, but my face was instantly apologetic. "I just want to get this over with, you know?"

Anna nodded, and I stepped into a pair of way-too-small Manolo Blahniks. The next place I found myself was at a restaurant looking at a woman who was sporting a colorful scrunchie.

"I dunno, all I'm sayin' is that you shouldn't rush into this kind of thing."

"I'm not rushing in, it's just that…I don't know, it seems like Richard was sent to me or something. And he's good to me."

Hearing my father's name in the context Meredith used it was off-putting. She was talking about him like he was…a man or something, not just a father.

The scrunchied woman took a sip of what looked like tomato juice and shook her head.

"He wasn't sent to you; he didn't find your lost glove at Saks and comb the world lookin' for you. He bought a couple of books from your bookstore. That doesn't mean anything."

"Yes, but that doesn't mean we weren't supposed to meet, Kathy. I mean, come on, he was buying *parenting* books. That's exactly what I want."

"What, a bratty kid to deal with? That's not what you want. You want to meet a nice guy, fall in love, get married and have that big hugging, kissing moment where you both rejoice over your new pregnancy. Then you wanna have a little girl, put pictures of Winnie the Pooh all over her pink walls and grow up to be best friends with her. I know I'm right, you don't have to tell me." She put up a hand and then took a bite of her pesto linguine.

Meredith shook her head, not having the energy to defend what she wanted. It might sound wonderful to have things play out the way Kathy had said, but what she really wanted was a child. Someone to help, someone who needed her, someone she could love unconditionally for the rest of her life.

"I mean, of course that would be wonderful…but

maybe this is good enough. After what I went through with Jim, I just don't think that I'll ever be able to make that fantasy happen."

"Jim," Kathy said with her mouth full, "was an ass-hole. Do you hear me? An ass-*hole.* Okay, he told you he wanted to get married and do all that, and then the second you go to the fertility doctor, he starts cheatin' on you with one of the nurses. That's how a lot of men are, let me tell you, but that doesn't mean that you should just settle for the next guy you meet."

"But *at* the doctor's, they told me I might not be able to have my own children." I felt the deep, aching sad-ness that washed over Meredith. She was so afraid that she wouldn't be able to have her own baby. I listened to her thoughts carefully, surprised at what they said. As far as I'd ever known, she was interested only in redecorating the house.

Her thoughts shifted back to the life that this guy Jim had promised her. She'd already painted the spare room in his house, back when she still lived there, and he'd called it "our house."

He'd told her that she was the one he'd been waiting for, and that he couldn't wait to see the baby they'd make together. And then she'd woken up in the middle of the night to sounds coming from the spare room, and opened the door to find Jim having sex with the fertility nurse.

And the nurse had been just that—fertile. She'd announced her pregnancy a month later, Meredith had heard.

She'd taken in the scene before her, shocked by all of the betrayals. Her fiancé, her nurse, her nursery, her Little Bo Peep lamp from her childhood illuminating their betrayal. The enormous insult that Jim hadn't even tried to be careful—he'd brought the nurse back to their home.

*With me,* Meredith thought, *sleeping naively in the other room.*

Meredith reasserted herself, bringing her thoughts back to her conversation with Kathy.

"But after all that...I mean maybe I *had* to be with Jim so that I could realize it isn't all going to play out like I thought it would. Maybe there is no Mr. Darcy." She smiled, weakly. "And Richard is no George Wickham, anyway; he's a really good person. The only problem he has is that he doesn't know how to deal with his daughter by himself. I can help them both."

Kathy looked intently at Meredith. "I dunno, Mer, I still think it's messed up to think of marrying a guy with a ten-year-old kid just because you think it *might* work out okay. I mean, you haven't said anything about how he makes you feel or anything. I'm no romantic or anything, you know that—" she laughed at the thought "—but, I mean, you guys have only *known* each other for six months."

"I realize that, but…"

"And, I'm sorry, but the very fact that he's talking about marriage already at this stage of the game is a turn-off." She crinkled her nose. "Isn't the kid a little snot, anyway?"

Meredith felt offended on my behalf.

"No, don't say that. She's just upset about her mother and she's become friends with the wrong crowd. That's all. She'll grow out of it, and I *know* that if I'm there for her at the right time, she'll turn out okay." She took a sip of her water. "Being raised by a nanny, like she is now, is just going to harm her in the long run."

Kathy clicked her tongue and opened her mouth to speak, but Meredith stopped her short.

"Listen, Kathy, please. He's got money, so I don't have to worry about security. He went through all of that stuff with his wife and she's been gone for a while now, leaving him to handle everything on his own. And Bridget…Bridget is a sweet girl. I've seen her have moments of kindness. She tries so hard with Richard…

and I don't know, there are moments where he seems to just resent his situation with her."

"Mmm. Sounds like a stand-up guy you've got there."

Meredith laughed humorlessly. "No, I don't mean it that way. I just think that he doesn't know how to handle her. I know he's upset about his wife, too, and I just think…that if anything, I can help both of them."

"I just don't see why you're giving up the dream of a real life and choosing to put yourself in the middle of somethin' that feels like a depressing storyline on *Guiding Light!* You're asking for more trouble than is worth it, I'm tellin' you." She looked at Meredith and softened. "But if this is what you wanna do, I'll be here for you, I will."

"Thanks, Kathy."

AND THEN THEY WERE GONE. The earth fell away, and the thunderous silence I'd grown accustomed to pounded in my ears.

When the noise ceased, I was standing in my father and Meredith's bedroom. It was before she'd decorated it and traded my mother's homey JCPenney-catalog style for a much more sleek and simple one.

My father was sitting at the foot of the bed, his head in his hands and elbows on his knees. It felt weird seeing him there in the house, he was there so rarely.

Meredith stood a few feet from him, leaning against the dresser. There was a tension in the air so strong you could almost taste it.

Meredith watched my father, not sure if she should say something or not. She didn't want to push him, didn't want him to get frustrated and say or do something he couldn't take back.

My father lifted his face from his hands and looked at Meredith. He looked disheveled and practically unlike himself. His dark hair, usually slicked back and trim-looking, was shaggy and hanging almost in the eyes that looked so much like mine. He was wearing a T-shirt and sweatpants and his expression was grim.

This was a while ago, I could tell. There were fewer lines around his eyes, and he looked less harsh. Since this scene, he and I had both changed.

"Meredith, I just don't know about this." He shook his head as he spoke.

"Richard, please. Please, you can't do this."

He studied her intently before looking out the window to his right.

What was happening? Was this a breakup? Surely it

couldn't have been so serious, since Meredith was still around.

She stepped away from the dresser and sat tentatively down on the bed with him.

"Listen, I know this is hard. It's really hard, but it's just how it is. It's not your fault, please understand that. It's how these relationships are." She waited for him to turn toward her and respond or at least react. He didn't. "There'll be fights and acrimony, and times when you feel like you just want to give up, but you can't *do* that. I promise you, it's just how this kind of thing goes."

"How do you know it's not me?" my father asked quietly, still gazing fixedly out the window.

Meredith gave a small laugh. "Because you stayed."

Oh, my *God,* he almost left her? The marriage almost ended?

A small, shameful thrill ran through me. Would my life have been better if he *had* left her?

It took only a moment to see the error of my thinking.

"How could she be okay after this?" my father asked.

*She?*

"Her mother's gone, and all she's got left is me, Mer. Me, and I'm not a good father—"

Oh, my God, he was talking about *me.*

"—I never have been. I never thought I would be, and here I am trying to raise a child on my own. I've been doing all right for these past few years, but…what happens when all the hard stuff comes around, huh? The boyfriends, the girl stuff…I just don't know how to handle that."

"No mother innately knows how to do that either, it's learned. Everyone has to learn how to do this stuff."

"Well then, how come you're so good at it?"

She relaxed as she heard the small hint of lightheartedness in his voice. He wasn't arguing with her, at least.

"I guess I picked up a few things with my sisters and their kids."

He gave a small smile, which quickly faded as his thoughts came back to him. He looked down into his lap and spoke. "Mer…I just don't know how to do this. I don't think I can."

What was he saying? That he was going to somehow get rid of me? Ship me off somewhere?

"I'll help you," Meredith said to him.

He looked up at her and considered her for a long time before asking, "You sure?"

She tilted her head at him, and nodded.

He took her hand, and then, just as I thought it would, the floor fell away.

I ASSUMED I WOULD END up in the boardroom, but I was back in the same restaurant as before, clearly at yet another time. Kathy had pulled her chair around to sit right next to Meredith, and had an arm around her.

I instantly felt the weight of an enormous disappointment that Meredith was carrying.

"I just can't believe it happened, you know? I mean I *can* believe it but, I just…hoped that it wouldn't…and, here I am…"

"I know, sweetie, I know," Kathy said, squeezing Meredith's shoulder a little too hard.

"I thought that it was real this time. I thought that after everything I've been through for the last ten years, that I'd…I just thought I deserved it." A swell of tears welled up in Meredith's eyes. I could feel her awareness of the other diners, and she tried to calm herself down.

"Did they say why it might have happened?" Kathy asked.

"Well, I mean we've known for a long time that it would be hard for me to carry a baby to term, but…" She sobbed again. "They checked my progesterone levels and they were fine this time, there was nothing in the amnio that would have suggested the baby wasn't..." She broke down in tears again. "*Viable.* That was the word they used. They don't know what happened except to say up to twenty percent of pregnancies end in miscarriage and I can try again." She gave a dry laugh. "Like this one didn't matter."

"It's that girl. It's the stress that's making this happen." Kathy took her arm back from around Meredith and started using it to gesture broadly. "I mean, first you've gotta deal with the teacher stuff, then you've gotta deal with Richard being out of town all the time, then you've gotta deal with her *constant* berating of you." She threw her hands up in the air. "I mean *what* is it gonna take, Mer? I don't mean to make you feel worse, but you have *got* to get out of that house. You tried it out for years, and it's just not working out. The child is un*fix*able. The husband is not there, ever. The house is all you've got, and if you brought in that Bridget to the divorce hearing as exhibit A, I bet they'd just give it to you for all your efforts."

"I can't just leave them, Kathy, it's exactly what her mother did."

My heart stopped for a moment. That was a low blow, to call my mother's car accident "leaving" us.

"Yeah, maybe she was smart. No mother should leave her kid, don't get me wrong, but you gotta see why, lookin' at that girl."

Smart? Was this woman suggesting that my mother committed *suicide* or something because of *me?* That wasn't at all true.

I felt Meredith's temper climb. But there was something else. An irritation not with Kathy's disrespect but with my mother. I couldn't understand that. How could she be *angry* with my mother for dying tragically?

"Kathy—"

"You know it's true, Meredith. The woman up and left her child and husband for a career as a *waitress* in *Vegas* for God's sake!" She snorted derisively. "A normal mother doesn't do that, but maybe the problem is that it's not a normal child."

"Enough, Kathy." Meredith's voice was sharp. "That was *not* Bridget's fault. Whatever else was, *that* wasn't. I never should have told you that. I didn't tell you so you'd have ammunition for an argument. I didn't tell you that so you could tell me that the decision I committed to is the wrong one." She stood. "I don't need you to tell me how difficult my life is. I know exactly how hard it is, and how challenging it's been trying to help raise Bridget. But you have *got* to understand that what her mother did was wrong, and that I would *never* do that to her."

I felt like I couldn't breathe. Like I was being drowned by my own thoughts. I couldn't even hear what was happening in Meredith's head anymore.

My mother *left?* I tried to wrap my mind around that concept. I'd always trusted my father implicitly, not thinking that I had any reason to do otherwise. Why did he tell me she was *dead?* Was that better than thinking she left?

I considered that for a moment and realized that might have been the one time my father had acted with implicit knowledge of who and how I was. If I'd known she'd left when I was younger, I don't think I could have taken it. I might never have been able to move beyond it.

Could I now?

I thought of the day with the fondue again. Where my mother and I had curled up on the sofa and watched my favorite movie and eaten my favorite food. She'd been okay with the movie, but I'd had to beg for the fondue—she didn't like all the fat it contained—but in the end we'd gotten it and the day had been so fun. So cozy.

Why?

*Why did she leave?*

I tried to think of a time when I was so bad that it would make her want to give up, but I couldn't remember anything. The only memories I had of my mother were fond ones.

Suddenly a wave of new revelations came over me. She'd never called or anything, she'd just let me believe she was dead. Did she know the story my father had come up with? Was she okay with it? Was that the deal they'd made, that she'd leave but agree never to contact me from beyond the made-up grave?

Or had she just left without any regard to the fallout? Maybe my father woke up one morning and she was gone. Maybe there was a fight and she left, slamming the door behind her, not giving a second thought to the daughter asleep upstairs. The daughter who expected to wake up in the morning to the chocolate milk that her mother always made perfectly.

Instead, she was gone.

And he'd had to come up with a story.

I felt betrayed, thinking of my parents. My father had lied to me for years now without ever hinting at the truth, even when I got older. And my mother had just left me. I was shocked to find that the only person it seemed I could trust was Meredith.

And I'd spend years treating her like the evil stepmother from *Cinderella.*

I was hardly paying attention to what was happening in Meredith's head as she walked up to our house. But I realized what must be coming next. She opened the door, thinking regretfully of her argument with Kathy.

Once the door was open, she saw me standing there with my arms crossed. Her stomach lurched, and she hoped I wouldn't try to argue with her. She saw the expression on my face, and was sure that she wouldn't be so lucky.

She knew me better than my own mother did.

She sighed and tried to think of how she could get me to understand that it wasn't the right time. "Listen, Bridget—"

"What did you guys talk about? Did you swap stories about how awful I am?"

Meredith's head throbbed at my words.

"Bridget, please." She walked to the love seat and sat down feeling profoundly tired. "Listen, I just can't talk about this right now."

"You can't just go off with *my* teacher and then refuse to tell me what happened, Meredith." My piercing voice echoed in the house.

"I'm not *refusing,* I just have other things on my mind, and—"

"If you'd just say it, this conversation would end so much sooner."

Meredith took a deep breath, feeling resigned.

"He's fed up with you being disrespectful," she quoted him. "You and he, he and I, you and I, have *all* had that conversation. It is just time you stop. You don't want to be removed from the class and have to take it again."

"Obviously," I said shortly.

Meredith cringed at the word. She wondered how I managed to sound so patronizing and so juvenile at the same time.

"Did he say that he might kick me out of the class?" I sounded so insistent. I was basically asking for a favor by asking her for information about a favor she'd already done.

And I had the *gall* to be this relentless.

Meredith felt herself reaching the end of her rope.

She couldn't do this right now; she just *couldn't* spend more energy on me. She spent most of the day doing that.

"He just mentioned it as being an option. Honestly, we only spoke for a few minutes."

"But you were gone for like, three hours."

"Yes, Bridget, I was doing other things." Meredith hoped I would stop there; hoped that she wouldn't have to open up to me and tell me what hell she'd been through. She could take me being inconsiderate about a lot of things, but this was too private.

"*What* were you doing?" I shouted at her.

Meredith's anger bubbled to the surface suddenly. "Enough!"

Fine. If I wasn't going to let this go, then I was going to get a fight.

Meredith mentally prepared herself for what she was going to ask me.

"Why are you like this, Bridget?"

"Why am I like what?"

"So rude, all the time! It doesn't matter if I try to help you, or if I try to do something nice, it's never *enough!* I've been in your life for the past seven years, and you *still* treat me like the evil stepmother. Last I remember, the biggest request I asked of you was to let *me* take you to go see a movie you wanted to see! And yet you sit here with your friends, and put me on the spot..."

She thought desperately of that morning. She'd thought that at the very least she had a baby on the way.

She'd thought that the rest of the things that happened were just obstacles of life.

She remembered the conversation with me in the kitchen. How I'd pushed her then, too, just like I had so many times.

"I don't even know what you're talking about—"

"I tried to leave the house today by simply saying I was off to meet someone. I didn't *want* to mention that I was going to have a meeting with Mr. Ezhno, because I was trying not to embarrass you!"

"Why should *I* be embarrassed? You two are the ones who keep meeting to—"

"Because, Bridget! You're too old for this. I can't believe your teachers are *still* calling parent-teacher meetings, just like they were when you were a kid! Usually, at this age, you would have earned independence and trust from your family by acting like an adult—or no, not even an adult. Just simply by acting your age, instead of trying to get attention by being the class clown and terrorizing your teachers and everyone else you go to school with."

Meredith looked at my gaping mouth. There was a weakening in my face that looked like *maybe* I would think about what she was saying.

"Well, maybe I was never taught manners. I mean,

the only mother I had died in a car accident, before you came to live here. *She* was the only one who ever *really* loved us, but she's gone and you've just taken over."

Meredith felt like she'd been slapped. Came to *live* here. Like she was just a hanger-on who'd come to mooch off my family.

She opened her mouth, longing to tell me the truth. That my mother *wasn't* dead. That she was somewhere in Nevada, leading an easy, Bridget-less life. To say that she, *Meredith,* was the one who'd been there for me. The one who'd defended me to teachers, other parents, other people. She thought of Kathy. The only time she'd ever fought with her, since they were children, was about me.

And I had no idea.

Meredith longed to demand that I appreciate everything she'd done, what she'd sacrificed, what she'd—she felt foolish even remembering it—hoped for. She closed her mouth, unable to bring herself to say what she was thinking. It had always been her flaw: She was never able to just tell off the people who needed it. Who deserved it.

"So obviously, if you're going to be all parental, I'm not the right one to do it with. And let's face it, it's not your thing." A shooting pain struck Meredith's stomach, wiping all other thoughts from her mind. As soon as the pain was gone, however, the combined feelings hurt even more.

Meredith watched me go up the stairs, feeling sick as she stood waiting for the shuttle that would arrive any minute. Maybe Bridget was right, she thought, after all...Meredith *had* been there for me, and I didn't even notice.

And look how I had turned out.

# CHAPTER THIRTEEN

I knew I was back in the boardroom when I felt my knees give out, sending me falling helplessly onto the ground. I didn't bother to stop myself. I wrapped my arms around my knees and threw my face onto my forearms. I wished I could hide in the red tunnel at the playground, where no one could see me. Except maybe Liam.

I knew Anna was probably watching me, but I didn't care. I couldn't. All I could think of was my mother, and the fact that she left me. The words kept hitting me again and again, like pounding on a door. I was sobbing, noiselessly. My stomach ached from being flexed with my crying.

I probably only sat there for a couple minutes, but

it felt like years. I sorted through all the reasons I felt betrayed by my mother. *My mother*...the words didn't even sound right anymore.

And she'd left before I'd ever even become my own person, before she'd even gotten to *know* me. Suddenly I was mad at her.

Memories rushed back. Ones I'd blocked out and replaced with fond ones. I remembered asking her to look at my art project, and her rolling her eyes and saying something like, "Great." Tugging on her pajamas in the morning, and telling her I felt sick, then her telling me to be quiet and let her sleep. To get ready for school.

The days she'd sent me to school without lunch or lunch money.

When I'd told her my shoes didn't fit anymore, and she'd told me to deal with it.

The day she'd gotten mad at me for having another glass of chocolate milk without asking, and she'd yelled at me that I'd been a mistake.

My father hadn't had any time for me. He'd been gone. He used to spend time with me when he *was* home, but then I'd pushed him away. I don't know why. I'd stopped laughing at his jokes and rolled my eyes every time he said anything to me.

I reveled in self-torture for a moment longer, and then eventually felt my weeping begin to subside. But then the other things that I'd just seen hit me like bullets.

Because of me, Brett got in trouble for cheating on the test, and has a suspension on his record.

Because of me, Mr. Ezhno was fired. Not fired from just any job, but from a job he'd been so passionate about.

Because of me, or at very, very least *partially* because of me, Michelle gagged herself after every meal.

Because of me, Liam had lost his best friend. Me. I'd spent so long thinking he was a jerk for dumping me out of the blue, after such a long history. But I could see now that I had changed.

A new wave of stomach-flexing tears came at me again. I could suddenly see myself as the nice girl I'd been. I'd been eager to please as a child, and I'd cared about things. I was quiet, and kind, and was perfectly content to play with a toy by myself. I didn't need anyone else, but I still liked when friends and family were around.

It's a shame, I thought, it's a waste. The grown-up equivalents of the things I'd done in my childhood were not measuring out equally. I had been happy with the toys I had, the books and movies and pretend games. I'd watch *Cinderella* over and over all day long, and love it every time. But when it came time to being happy with my car, my friends, my very existence, I had to either show it off or complain about it not being good enough. Or turn it bulimic.

Because of me, my father had stopped trying.

Because of me, my mother had left.

I thought of what Meredith had said, that it wasn't my fault she left. And maybe it wasn't entirely. Considering the way I thought of my mother now—as a stranger—there was every chance that she wasn't the angel I'd thought. But what I hadn't realized was that Meredith *had* been there. Even if my mother *had* died, Meredith had done a huge thing, coming into my family the way she had and being so optimistic about everything.

*That* was the worst thing I'd done. I'd wronged Meredith. It wasn't that Anna showed me that my mother had left to simply make me feel bad about myself. It was to show me that Meredith was the real saint. And she deserved better.

And for the first time that I could remember, I felt really remorseful. Not just guilty because I got caught doing something, or because it ultimately ended up screwing me over in the end. I felt the weight of *everything* I had done. I could suddenly see the grenade effect of my own actions.

It was like Anna had said, I was important. My actions mattered. But I was realizing something…I wasn't *more* important.

It's not that I ever consciously thought it mattered more if I was happy than if someone else was happy. I don't think. Only that I didn't think that something I said in passing might affect someone so much.

My tears subsided again, and I was shocked to realize that I felt okay. Well maybe not *okay*…I felt repentant, like I finally realized that I had done a lot of wrong. I felt like I had been, well, a total bitch.

And often.

But I also felt like I was ready to spring into action. I knew what I'd done wrong, and I really wanted to fix it. I finally felt like the kind of grown-up version of little me—which is how it's supposed to be. I felt like I was finally open to being okay with myself, and that meant that I was finally going to be able to just… fix it.

But was that possible?

I lifted my head from my lap, my face hot and wet.

I coughed, feeling sheepish after my sobfest, and lifted myself off the ground to sit down in the chair behind me. I cleared my throat again.

"So." I looked up to Anna, and realized that all six of the people in front of me were now looking at me. It was disconcerting. Like statues turning to look at you.

"They're only here to help deliberate. They won't hear you."

I kept my eyes on them, unsure what to think. They were here, but…they weren't. It was like seeing someone in a casket—they're still there, and that's a weird feeling, but there's something vital missing. Not vital like a heartbeat…but a kind of spirit.

"I don't…really know what to say. I know what I've done…and I want to fix things. But I don't know what happens now."

"Well, now you've seen why you're here. You should have seen, at least, an explanation for what has landed you here."

"Where is 'here?'" I knew I sounded desperate.

Anna shrugged. "Nowhere, everywhere, take your pick. It doesn't really have a name." She gave a small laugh that I didn't understand.

"Is it like limbo or something?" My heart skipped a

beat as I remembered when my father had told me that the real meaning behind J. M. Barrie's story of *Peter Pan* was that Neverland was purgatory. I'd always hated that thought. I liked it much better when it was just an adventure.

"In a way."

"Please just tell me what I have to worry about."

Anna considered me for a moment. "We're deciding whether you're going to go back to that life—" she tilted her head and smiled knowingly "—or not."

My heart sank. They were deciding whether I was going to live or die. The scenes that had flashed through my mind during those last few moments in the car were back.

The news of my demise.

The funeral.

The headstone. It would have my name, and the years in which I'd been alive. The brief elapsed time that encompassed my entire existence. The drama, the friends, the makeup, Liam…

"Please, just wait!" The grenade was on the verge of exploding. "Anna, please, I think I know what might… happen here. And I just…I have to do something."

"Tell me what you mean." Anna sat back in her chair and waited for me to respond.

I scrambled to think of what I could do.

"Just…let me go back."

Anna raised her eyebrows. I shook my head.

"Not, like, permanently or whatever. Just…I can't leave all of these people…" I looked at them "…all of you…them…to think this way. It's not fair to them. I can't take it all back, or undo what I did, but there must be something I *can* do."

Anna paused. She looked slightly more intimidating than I'd originally thought her to be. "Why should we believe that you'd be able to do anything at all?"

"I—" My heartbeat quickened as I realized that I really might not get a second chance. I didn't just get my way anymore. "Well, take Meredith, for example. She doesn't think she'd be a good mother anymore, and that's because of me. Even if it was just a fleeting thought, she's already been discouraged because of all the failed attempts. If I die—" my voice caught on the word. Death had always seemed such a foreign thing "—If I die and this is how we left things…I don't know, I think she'd feel even worse. Maybe she'd even think that it was partially her fault. She managed to think the rest of it was, and it just wasn't. It was all mine."

I thought, with a stab of guilt, of my last thoughts behind the wheel. Part of me had actually *hoped* that Meredith would feel partially responsible.

Anna narrowed her eyes.

"What if she feels relieved?"

Her frankness felt like a cheap shot.

"She might." I knew it was true. There was every chance that Meredith would feel less stress with me gone. I looked down to my lap. "But I have to try. With all of them. Closure, and all that."

"And if we allow this…breach, you'll fix what you can, and then come quietly?"

I nodded. "Yes."

"We'll have to discuss it." She and the others stood swiftly, leaving their pads on the table, and walked into a room I was sure hadn't been there before.

I don't know how long they were gone, but it felt like a very long time. I didn't look at the pads, which were filled in now with a lot of things I couldn't fully read from my seat. I saw my name, and yearned to see what Liam had written.

But I was acting with a conscience now. And I wouldn't go read them.

Instead, I replayed everything I'd just seen in my

mind. Tried to remember why I'd thought my actions were *not* entirely inconsiderate. Worried desperately about the things they were saying behind the door that had, once again, disappeared.

It was that feeling that happens at night when you're trying to fall asleep but all you can think about is all of the things you need to do. You can't do anything about them yet, and it helps nothing to think obsessively about it. Yet you can't stop and relax.

When the six of them finally emerged from the room, my heart seemed to jump into my throat. I tried to look kind and as remorseful as I felt, though I was sure that the decision was made and that I couldn't do anything about it.

They took their seats, and Anna looked at me.

"You have until midnight, at which point you will either have completed your task or not. You don't get any help from…elsewhere. The consequences of your actions are, as you've probably imagined, irrevocable. Do you understand?"

Yes, I understood. And I didn't care what happened to me anymore. I just had to fix what I'd done to everyone else.

"Midnight," she repeated firmly. "Then it's over. Time's up. Got it?"

I nodded at Anna, and the second I did so, I felt like I'd been hit in the head with a frying pan. My eyes shut, and I felt like my whole body was being squeezed through some sort of wringer.

# CHAPTER FOURTEEN

The next thing I knew, I was in the bed at the nurse's office. I looked around me, and there was no one there. The clock on the wall said it was 12:45. I had eleven hours and fifteen minutes until midnight.

I got up from the leather bed and walked up to the front of the office.

"Ah, Miss Duke, better already?"

"Yes, I'm better."

"Let's get you on to class then. I'll fill out a pass."

I watched as she filled out the lines on the pink slip of paper. When she finished, she handed it to me. "Here you go."

"I'm sorry for all of the times I've come in here."

"Excuse me?" She looked puzzled.

"Just…I've come in a lot, and I'm sorry. It's annoying, I'm sure."

I closed the door on her puzzled expression and ran to gym class, to the girls' locker room. Once there, I made a beeline toward Michelle's and my lockers.

I was only a few minutes late.

I took a deep breath before walking over to her. I didn't know exactly how to go about this.

"Hey, Michelle!"

She turned, and looked tiredly at me.

"Hey."

This was going to take work. "So," I started, "we should do something this weekend. I haven't really seen you one on one too much lately."

"Oh, yeah. Okay." She opened her locker and pulled out her gym shorts, looking warily at them as she did so. I pulled out mine, too.

"Did you know that my gym shorts are size extra large?" I said, dialing the combination to my lock.

Michelle looked at me, and I nodded. "Yep. Last pair left. And you know what's bad? I'm able to wear them! But I mean, the gym clothes here run really small anyway."

"You think?" Michelle's voice sounded hesitantly hopeful.

I really hoped she kept being this easy to convince.

"Of course, yeah. Size small might as well read 'six to eight months,' it's so tiny. But I mean, you probably didn't notice that, you're what, like a size triple zero?"

"Size two." She said it sadly, like she was telling me that no, in fact, she wore size circus tent.

I cringed at the idea that I'd contributed to that unhealthy attitude. "Same thing," I said, my tone casual.

I wanted to wait a few minutes before starting my apology. I wanted to be sure it didn't look like what I'd said about the shorts was just a prelude to making myself feel better. Because, really, it wasn't. The shorts really were ridiculously small for the most part.

We headed out to the track, where we were on our third week of running around it. There were different classes you could sign up for to qualify for a gym credit. This one had been called Dance but so far all we'd done was "become strong young women, who will have the fortitude to become dancers." The teacher had then reminded all of us that if we had really been interested in dance, we would have started in our early childhoods, and that we were too late anyway.

Michelle and I ambled behind the rest of the class at our usual pace.

"Hey, so, by the way," I started, my heart beating hard, "I wanted to apologize to you."

I looked straight ahead, but I could feel Michelle's eyes shift to me.

"For what?"

"Well, I was a bitch the other day when you tried to talk to me. I'm really bad with being told I'm wrong about things."

"I didn't say you were wrong about anything."

"But I was, Michelle, I shouldn't have ever made you feel bad about yourself. There's nothing to feel bad about, for one thing, and for another…that's crappy friend behavior on my part."

Michelle stared at me. I hadn't really noticed until that moment that we'd stopped moving. I looked at her, trying to look as sincere as I felt.

"Listen, when we were kids you were always the prettiest girl at school. Everyone loved you, and you were every guy's first crush. I've always been jealous of the fact that you didn't even have to do anything to get people to like you, and it hasn't been fair how I've acted, but you've got to understand that any time I've ever said anything mean to you about your looks or anything else…it's just because I'm totally jealous of you. And I'm just really sorry."

"Bridget," Michelle started, looking confused, "I don't know exactly what I should say, I mean…since when?"

"Like, forever? Look, it's just that I did hear you the other day when you said you were feeling insecure, and I just want to do anything I can to show you that you completely don't need to be."

She looked at me intently for a moment, before looking down at her tennis shoes.

"Bridget, there's something I've been meaning to tell you."

I nodded encouragingly, hoping that she would confide in me.

"It's kind of hard to say, I guess." She looked at me. "But I just don't think we can be friends anymore."

My breath caught in my throat. I had no idea what to say. I shouldn't have been so surprised. She was just telling me what she'd probably been advised by any *better* friends to say sooner.

I remembered how she'd felt watching me at my party. It wasn't quite admiration, and it wasn't bitterness. It was more like an entirely objective observation. She had noticed how people felt about me, and she knew how people acted around me. Or used to. She knew about my effect on people, but it didn't stretch to her.

I also realized that I really was used to things working out the way I wanted them to. It wasn't that I asked for money and it rained from the skies or anything. Only that things usually went my way. If I needed a favor from someone, I usually got it. I'd been told no before, but it didn't matter because I always knew I'd get a yes in the end.

But it wasn't going to work this time. She wasn't just going to accept my apology and say that she understood. We weren't going to plop down on the grassy hill we stood on and talk about how to get her through her bulimia. There wouldn't be any hand-holding. There wouldn't be any crying. And it looked like there wouldn't be any regret on Michelle's end.

I nodded and stood there like my feet were planted in the ground, and she walked away, headed toward the track.

I looked up to see her running her hands through her hair, the way she did when she was confident. She wasn't standing up with her stomach sucked in and her shoulders in a shrug. She strode confidently across the field.

I smiled. Maybe I did get what I wanted.

After gym class, which had that awkward post-breakup feel that seemed to give me a taste of how the rest of the year would be if I were to be there, I went to the main office.

"I need to speak to the headmaster. Please."

The secretary nodded, and picked up the phone. After a brief moment of lowering her tinny voice and looking indiscreetly in my direction, she told me to have a seat in the waiting room and he'd be with me momentarily.

I nodded and marched over to the chairs I was so accustomed to.

Sure enough, Vince, the guy who was always there, sat in his usual seat.

I drew in a deep breath, keeping the words *How are you ever in class long enough to get in trouble* in my mouth. I smiled curtly and sat down in the seat that I figured gave me the least eye contact with him.

"What're y'in for?" he asked suddenly.

"Um. I just have to talk to Ransic about some stuff." I looked at my hands quickly, wishing I'd brought a magazine, and then realized that the boardroom wasn't exactly lousy with them.

"Gotcha."

I bit my lip uncomfortably and decided to take another step toward being a more caring person.

"What about you? What are you, um, in for?"

"Oh, I dunno, I flipped over some kid's lunch tray." His voice was gruff, and he sounded almost exactly like my dad's mechanic friend. He may as well have been saying, "Oh, I dunno, it'll take y'a couple hundred, maybe a thou."

"Why?"

"Dumbass walked right in fronna me."

I thought for a moment of whether I should ask my next question. I decided I should. "So what?"

"So what?" He put his hands on his thighs and leaned toward me. "So what? I hate when people don't watch where they're goin'."

I nodded, as if I understood, and pointed my gaze toward the wall to my left. I heard him chuckle, and turned back to look at him. "What?"

"Well, I dunno, I guess I just think it's funny. You. Me."

I let out a derisive snort. "What about—" I hesitated, not wanting to use the word *us* "—you or me?"

"Well, I guess we're kinda runnin' the same game here. Don't you think?"

"I don't know what you mean." I tried to say

it with that "end of the conversation" tone, but it didn't work.

"Well, you keep all the girls in line, and I do the same for the dudes. And the freshmen."

"What are you *talking* about?"

"Haven't you noticed what happens when you walk down the hallway? Do people jump outta your way, not wantin' to mess with you?" He beamed at my blank expression, as if it was what he'd expected. "Yeah, they do, I've seen it. "

I gawked at him, not wanting to admit that this guy had me pinned.

"But I still don't think that makes us alike. No offense, but you just bully everyone. I don't do that."

"Hey, you might not take money from 'em, but you do even more than that." He leaned back and shut his eyes, signaling that he was finished talking to me.

But I was pulling out the bitch card once more. "Hey, Vince." He opened his eyes, and I fastened the expression I'd mastered for this sort of thing. "I get what you're saying. It's not just the girls who listen to me. So here's what you're going to do. You're going to stop. Stop messing with people. It's been pissing me off for a while, and I've had enough. If you flip over any more lunch trays, or steal any more money—" I smiled as cunningly as I could "—then you're going to deal with *me*."

"Yeah? What are you going to do to me?"

"Oh, I've got a plan. And I know you're fond of this school, considering how long you've been here. So, really, if you don't stop? You're going to find yourself repeating your senior year at the local public school." One last jab. "Plus, you're just annoying, you're not even scary."

I was just winging it, and was terrified he was going to call me out. To tell me I was full of it, and that he wasn't afraid of me. Instead he just sat back in his chair again and shut his eyes. But there was the smallest of creases between his eyebrows that told me that just *maybe* I'd done something right.

But as I sat there, my heart sank as I realized that maybe he was right. I might *not* take their money, but I did take their self-esteem. My heart sank lower as I thought of Mr. Ezhno and his job—that was unquestionably worse that what Vince did. I was taking so much more from Mr. Ezhno than just his money.

Maybe Vince and I *were* the same. Only he was even further along than I was—because at least he *knew* what he was, without being told by some mystical judge in a boardroom.

That thought put everything into perspective, even more than the thought of my life being on the line.

After fifteen minutes, the headmaster called me into his office. The look on his face told me very clearly that he didn't want to deal with me anymore.

"Sit." He spoke shortly, pointing halfheartedly toward the chair he was passing.

I sat obediently and waited for him to sit down.

"Listen, Mr. Ransic, I have a few things to tell you. And I don't really know how—"

"Just say it, Miss Duke. I've got things to do here, and I don't need you quibbling over how to perfectly phrase your newest problem."

Something in his voice made me picture him getting home from work, throwing down his briefcase and talking to his girlfriend about what a stressful day he'd had. I pictured her asking what had happened. He would sink down into an armchair, and talk about "this *girl*" at school with all these *problems*.

I shook the scenario from my head and started with what had happened with Brett.

"Okay, so Brett Cooper didn't do anything wrong."

The headmaster drew in an exasperated breath before asking, "Pardon?"

"Brett wasn't the one who was cheating, I was, and I just said everything I said because I didn't want to get in trouble."

He looked like he was trying to remember the details of the incident.

"Look," I said, "I just don't want him to get in trouble. I lied, and he shouldn't get in trouble for it."

"What are you up to, Miss Duke?"

"Nothing. Really. It's just that what I did was wrong, and I feel bad about it. So can't you just, like, unsuspend him or something?"

He studied my face, looking for an explanation for my sudden honesty.

"Look, Miss Duke, I don't know why you're saying this, but he's already on his first day of suspension, and there's really not much I can do."

"What are you talking about? You're the headmaster, you can do whatever you want!"

I gazed at him with hopeful, wide eyes. He looked skeptically back at me.

"Do you realize that you're going to be punished in his place? That this isn't going to be some act of kindness you're doing, and it won't all just go away?"

I held back a *duh*.

"Yes, of course." I nodded stoically.

He shook his head and took off his glasses.

"You said there were 'some things' you wanted to discuss. Is there something else?"

"Mr. Ezhno."

"What about him?"

"He's been fired, right?"

"Mr. Ezhno will no longer be teaching here," he confirmed, looking as though he was choosing his words carefully.

"Right. Well, that's my fault, too."

The headmaster put his elbows on his desk and his face in his hands, the way he had when I'd seen him through Brett's eyes.

"What?" he said into his hands. I could hear his annoyance, even though his voice was muffled.

"Um. My friends misconstrued something I said… and really, Mr. Ezhno hasn't done anything wrong at all." I raised my hands and contorted my face into an expression meant to read *So, really, it's all just a big misunderstanding!*

"Miss Duke, this is all seeming a little far-fetched for me. How am I supposed to believe everything you're saying when part of what you're saying is that I shouldn't believe anything you've said?"

"Because it makes no sense for me to lie about having

done these things! I'm only getting myself into trouble. You *know* it's not like me to do that if I don't have to."

He opened his mouth and then shut it again.

I scooted to the front of my chair.

"Okay, listen, I know this all sounds really weird, but you have to just help me fix this. I did all of this stuff wrong, and people's lives are being *ruined*. Brett and Mr. Ezhno shouldn't have to get in trouble just because of me."

"Well, of course not."

"Right," I said, taken aback by his vehement agreement. "Um. So, if you could just fix this stuff with Brett, and then if you could just hire back Mr. Ezhno, that'd be awesome. At this point *you're* the only one who can help me to make it right."

I knew it sounded ridiculous asking for so much, and I knew he knew it, too. But he looked at me and nodded.

"Fine. But you're in trouble, Miss Duke. You must understand the gravity of what you've done. This is serious. You've put Mr. Cooper, Mr. Ezhno and myself in a real spot."

"I realize that, and I'm sorry. If there was something I could do to take it back I would. Or if there's something

I can do to help *now* I will, but I don't know if there is. Besides what I'm doing, I mean."

He looked like he couldn't think of another solution, either.

"All right, well, I suppose you're right. There isn't much more you can do. But, I'm telling you, Miss Duke…" He looked me in the eyes and held up a finger. "…there will be disciplinary repercussions for what you've done. Finish out the day and come back here in the morning with a parent or guardian to sort out the extent of it. Stop at Miss Talley's desk and she'll give you a pass to class."

I nodded my head and stood to leave. I stopped at the door as I noticed that the wood-paneled walls looked almost identical to the ones in the boardroom.

"Is there something else? Hunger in the third world? Was that you, too?"

"Oh. No, sorry." I took one last look at the wall, then went to Ms. Talley for a hall pass that I might or might not need where I was going.

# CHAPTER FIFTEEN

The day continued on in a strangely normal way. I spent the whole time feeling like I could be snatched out of reality and taken to Anna's boardroom at any moment, but in the meantime I had to continue to do everything I could to help the people I'd hurt.

It rained heavily as I drove—slowly and carefully—home from school, my windshield wipers working furiously to keep the rain from obscuring my vision. Once home, I was relieved to see that Meredith's car was in the driveway. I parked quickly and pounded up the front steps.

"Meredith?" I called the second I walked through the door. It felt strange calling her name, and I wondered if I'd ever actually shouted it this eagerly before.

When I found her she was in the basement with Todd, the ever-present interior decorator. He was wearing a lime-green polo shirt with a pair of butt-hugging jeans, and a pair of what looked like alligator-skin shoes. Neon green.

The two of them were discussing chair rails, and I decided that I had better just head back upstairs and wait until she was finished.

"Bridget?" Meredith spotted me.

"Hi, Meredith." I stopped. "Hey, Todd. I didn't see your car outside."

"Oh, no, my wife dropped me off."

I think I actually did a double take like Scooby-Doo does when something surprising happens. "Your *what?*"

"My wife, Janet."

He stood facing me with his hands on his lower back like a pregnant woman. I tried to take in his gelled, blond-tipped hair, the way he said all of his words like they were really exciting—even "chair rail"—and his overall flamboyancy and picture him with a wife. I had been one hundred percent sure he was gay.

"Oh, I didn't know you were, um, married," I said, trying not to sound as completely baffled as I was.

I looked at Meredith who was, I was pleased to see, stifling a giggle.

"Going on four years, yeah! So, Mer, let's get back to refinishing this *basement!*"

"Hey, Meredith, can I talk to you when you're finished here?"

"Is everything all right?"

"Sort of…I mean, yeah, I just have to talk to you, is all."

She stared concernedly at me for a moment and then nodded.

I went upstairs and sat down at the kitchen table, and stared fixedly at the wax fruits in the centerpiece.

I felt nervous. More nervous to talk to Meredith than I felt about the fact that I could very well be dead in a few hours. I looked at the clock. Three o'clock. I thought, sadly, of how many times I'd still been at school at this time in the afternoon. Thought of all the memories I had of sitting outside on the lawn, flirting with Liam or another boy (though the other ones weren't half as much fun), or joking around with Michelle and Jillian, planning what we were going to do for the rest of the day, and all the other things that had happened.

They all felt tainted now.

Maybe I'd been the only happy one, and everyone else had just been humoring me out of fear that I'd make their lives even more miserable than I already had. I felt like a fool, thinking I was making memories that would last forever, when all the while everyone had abhorred my very presence.

How many times had they left me and I'd gone off feeling happy while they'd exchanged wide-eyed, conciliatory looks about how dreadful or bitchy or selfish I was?

I didn't even want to know.

But there must have been times where they had fun, too, I reasoned. Why else would they have stayed friends with me? Just merely to avoid my, I don't know, *wrath?*

Surely not.

Right?

I didn't go after girls and laugh in their faces. I just talked about them, decided who was cool and who was not, and a number of other things that didn't make sense even to me anymore.

Then another thought struck me: Was Jillian still my friend?

Maybe not. I mean, who knew where her friendship loyalty really was?

I appreciated the irony in what was happening to me. I'd spent years making up for the embarrassments of my childhood and trying to make sure I didn't have any during high school. I had tried so hard to ensure that I had friends, and that my reputation stayed golden. But because of *how* I'd tried, I had been working slowly backward.

I thought of Mr. Ezhno and his optimism on the first day of school. And how I'd promptly proceeded to spend every class period teasing him and making it all harder for him. I wasn't the only one who did it, but I certainly contributed to it.

I hoped that what I'd done to start fixing everything was enough. Not enough to save my life, I was certain, but enough to help put things the right way again. Brett wouldn't be in trouble anymore, Mr. Ezhno would have his job back and Michelle would, hopefully, carry on with a little more confidence and try to get some help.

Then there's Meredith. What could I say or do that would be enough to undo what I'd done? At school I was just the person who filled everyone's quota for bitchy high school girl. But at home I was part of someone's life. Meredith had had some idea what she wanted for her future. And what she'd ended up with was me.

Then something hit me. Something that made me feel not only angry with myself and remorseful for my actions, but disappointed in myself.

I'd spent years fancying myself to be Cinderella.

Well, I had the story right, but the role wrong. It wasn't that Meredith was the evil stepmother—I was the evil stepdaughter.

The thought shook me.

I pulled my phone out of my purse, pressed the three on speed dial and held it, shaking, to my ear. It rang. Rang some more. Then it went to voicemail.

*You have reached the voicemail box of*—the recording skipped and I heard my father's voice—*Richard Duke. Please press one—*

I pressed one. The phone beeped, and I spoke.

"Um, hey, Daddy…it's um, it's Bridget. I haven't talked to you in forever, or seen you at all…I just…I just wanted to say…" What did I want to say? Neither my dad nor I were sappy, emotional people. We didn't talk about our feelings. And I couldn't tell him what I'd learned about my mom. He'd wanted me to believe she was dead for a reason. I took a deep breath. "When you're back in town next time, I think we should hang out. It's been too long since we've talked, and—" I chose honesty "—I've just realized I've been kind of a total jerk for a while. So. I'm trying to make up for that. Call me back if you want to. Um. I love you. 'Bye."

Would I be dead when he called back? *If* he called back?

Just then, I heard Meredith's and Todd's laughing voices coming up the stairs.

"So we'll get started on that ASAP, right?" Todd said, his high voice sharpening on every *s* in his sentence.

"Absolutely, yes, just give me a call once you've figured out the colors and all, and we'll go look for the rest together. All right?" She smiled, and they walked amicably to the front door.

I watched as Meredith said goodbye and closed the door. There was an abrupt change in the atmosphere. The kind that always happens when the door closes on a guest and there's someone waiting for an argument or a conversation on the other side.

She strode into the kitchen toward the refrigerator.

"You want one?" She asked, holding up a pink Vitaminwater. Connect.

"Yeah, sure." I was feeling all of those things that sick or elderly people must feel when they're coming to the end of their lives. They must wonder if this will be the last time they see their grandchildren. Or if they're having their own last supper. Here I was, wondering if this was going to be my last fruity drink.

Meredith grabbed one for me and one for herself and pulled out the chair next to mine.

"You said you wanted to talk?"

Here it was.

"Yeah…okay, so I'm just going to launch right into my apology." I watched a crease come and go between her eyebrows after I said the last word. I took a deep breath. "So. I've been awful. For, like, the whole time I've known you. And it's not fair, I'm sorry."

Her expression was cautious. Dubious. "Bridget, where is this coming from?"

"Just that I know that I've been really mean to you. I can't undo everything I've ever said or done. And I really, truly don't expect you to accept my apology. But everything you said the other day was right. I can't act this way, and it's true that I've been acting really immaturely. Even cruel."

"Well, I—"

"Just don't say anything for a minute, okay? Please? Not like, because I don't care, but I have to just say what I'm saying before I lose my nerve, or my thoughts." *Or my life.*

Meredith agreed, looking bemused. I drew in several deep breaths, as I tried to think of how to explain what I was feeling.

"I realize now that you have been nothing but kind to me, and that all you've gotten in return is…me. And that's not fair; I've been such a jerk. I don't know what it is, but I've been sort of working things out in my life and I just want you to believe me when I say that it's not just you I've treated this way. It's not that I've ever thought or think now that there's anything wrong with you. You've been a great mother."

The burning sensation that indicates that tears are on their way had started about halfway through my speech.

Meredith's face had since softened, and she was now looking sympathetically at me.

"Bridget, honey, don't cry. It's okay, I understand."

"How could you understand? How can you accept my apology after how I've behaved?" My voice was pleading.

Meredith laughed. "Because I can tell that you mean it. There have been moments in our time together where I've believed I was seeing the real you. Do you remember when I picked you up from Outdoor Ed?"

I nodded.

"That was one of them," she said. "I knew you weren't trying to pull that trick on Michelle, that's why I never told your father. Although it turned out the camp director called him anyway." I felt my cheeks grow hot as she went on. "And I know that you've been sorting out who you want to be for a while."

"But I've been *such* a bitch!" I said the words with the same tone of disbelief an outsider might use after watching me for a while. Which was kind of how I felt.

"Listen, if you really want to change—and we all have to at different points in our lives—then just do it. And don't spend time worrying about whether or not the rest of the world is going to forgive you. Even if nobody you know wants to forgive you, you'll find new people. And you'll treat those people the way you've learned to."

The tears became harder to hold back as I listened to her speak. She was so much more compassionate than I could ever have been in a situation like this.

"Okay." I sniffled.

"And Bridget? I *totally* thought Todd was gay until he showed up today with his wife."

"Right?" I gave a small laugh, and hung in that

middle area between crying and laughing for a few minutes.

When I finally shook off the tears and simply sat there with puffy eyes, she told me that she had to run over to the store and asked if I'd like to come.

"Sure," I said, feeling genuinely excited to spend some nice time with her.

She smiled and told me that she just had to go change, and that she'd be back down in a minute.

I felt really happy to have her there. I didn't know anyone else who would have been that understanding about what I'd done. All the damage I'd caused. And she was good-natured enough to let bygones be just that. It takes a really, really strong person to do that.

As I washed my face of the tears and heavy mascara—which was all over my face—I felt really sorry. Not just because of everything I'd done, but also because I wished I had more time to fix it. I was going to be dead in only a few hours, and there was nothing I could do to stop it.

MEREDITH AND I WENT TO the grocery store and ambled around, picking up some vegetables, milk and other boring groceries that always seemed to be on the don't-forget-to-buy list. But I'd never felt more appreciative of the little things.

We were passing an endcap when I heard Meredith coo.

"Ooh, you know what would be awesome on a day like this? Fondue."

My mental jaw dropped at the suggestion. Meredith had meant on a cold, rainy day like this. But she didn't know what kind of day it was for me, or how right she was that it was exactly what we needed.

"Yeah, definitely."

Meredith tossed two boxes in the cart and grabbed two baguettes, saying, "Always better to have *more* than is healthy or necessary."

I laughed, still feeling shocked at the way the afternoon was playing out. "Hey, um. When was the last time you watched *The Sound of Music?*"

"Oh, man," she said, looking like she was thinking back a long way, "I don't think I've seen it since I was a kid. My mother and I used to watch it."

Huh.

"Do you want to watch it this afternoon?" I asked, feeling like I was asking someone on a date.

"Sure. I have a few things to do when we get home, but after that, definitely."

"Yeah, I have some stuff to do, too." I thought of Brett and Mr. Ezhno, and of course, my impending death.

When we got home I helped put away the groceries, despite Meredith's insistence that I didn't have to, and then ran up the stairs to the desk in my room.

Bypassing my laptop, I grabbed a pen and ripped some notebook paper out of my school binder, and sat down to write.

After several failed attempts, which resulted in a cartoonish mountain of balled-up pieces of paper, I had my first letter.

Mr. Ezhno,

There isn't much more I can say than I'm sorry. I've been a terrible student/person, and you've been a great teacher. I'm sorry for the snarky comments, I'm sorry for never getting to your class on time, I'm sorry for distracting other students who are trying to pay attention. And I'm really sorry that you got fired. For the record, I didn't intend for that to happen, and the whole thing was a misunderstanding set in motion by something stupid that I said. I told all of this to the headmaster, and he assured me that you'd get your job back.

Sincerely,

Bridget Duke

P.S. I'm sorry.

I read it to myself several times. It still didn't sound good enough, but ultimately I decided that it just couldn't sound good enough. There *was* no "good enough" for this kind of thing and even if there was, there wasn't time.

I folded it up and put it in an envelope, and started on my second letter. After even more failed attempts, I ended up with something I thought said it all.

Dear, dear Brett,

I'm so sorry.

Sincerely,

Bridget Duke

President of the Bitch Club

I took both letters, and put them in the middle of my bed. It wasn't like I'd be sleeping in it again, and I was sure that Meredith would get the letters where they needed to go.

MEREDITH AND I SPENT the rest of the afternoon doing what, I realized, we could have been doing for years.

We watched *The Sound of Music,* agreed that Liesl was too good for Rolf, who always seemed like a weasel and were glad we'd gotten two baguettes and boxes of fondue. The whole thing carried on as if we'd been doing it forever, and the entire time all I could think was how lucky I was that she would not only accept my apology, but that she would do anything with me at all. The second thought that floated through my mind was an echoing voice of warning, reminding me not to get too comfortable.

After Meredith and I parted ways for the evening, I took a phone outside and prepared for my last apology.

Or was it really my last goodbye?

I dialed Liam's cell phone number, which was still branded into my brain, and waited.

*Ring.*

Would he act like Michelle or like Meredith?

*Ring.*

Or would he just act like himself and politely say that he accepted, but feel like nothing had really changed?

*Ring.*

How could I show him that I really was different?

*Ring.*

What if—

"Hello?"

"Liam!" I shouted with relief.

"Hey, B, what's goin' on? Y'okay?"

He must be asking because I haven't actually *called* him in months.

"Yeah, no, everything's fine. But I do need to talk to you."

"I'm kinda on the way out the door right now. Can we talk in school tomorrow?"

Crap. He was putting the conversation on neutral territory. And impossible time.

"I'm not going to be there tomorrow. Listen, it's urgent, and I must talk to you face to face. Is there some way we can talk? Please, Liam."

"It's the homecoming game tonight, Bridge, I'm starting." He paused. "All right, are you going to the game?"

Well, now I am. "Yes."

"Talk to me after. But I'm warning you, Bridge—" his words made my heart jump "—I'm either gonna be *real* happy or *real* pissed."

I relaxed at the tone of his voice. He was kidding.

He knew something was wrong, and he wasn't being an asshole.

"I can handle it. Just meet me at the sideline benches as soon as the game is over."

"Okay, I'll talk to you then."

"Oh, Liam? What time's the game start again?"

"Eight. You weren't planning on going, were you?"

"See you later, Liam." My voice had a playful edge to it that I hadn't heard in a long time.

I looked at the clock again. Seven-thirty. Just—I counted on my fingers—four and a half hours and then I'd be gone.

How would it happen? Would a car hit me? Brain aneurysm? Heart attack at such a young age? Would I just…disappear, and find myself in the boardroom, sentenced to spend the rest of the eternity in hell or heaven?

IT WAS THE LAST FEW SECONDS of the game, and I'd spent the entire time up until then right on the sidelines shouting at the players.

As a child, my father had taught me the rules of every game known to man. He, like so many fathers, had wanted and expected me to be a boy. When I wasn't, he'd tried desperately to get me interested in sports. But the closest I got was the hissy fit I threw for Tennis Barbie.

And the cheerleading debacle.

But the knowledge had gotten me far with boys, and I'd been able to impress them with my sporty prowess. I'd walk through a room at a party, ask who was playing, and they'd give me some babyish answer about how the team from Washington was playing the team from Dallas. And I'd shoot back, "No, dumbass, I mean who's starting?"

But on this particular night, I had started off on my own. I had no friends to meet anymore, so I walked straight down the metal stadium stairs, my low heels banging like snare drums with every step I took.

I waved and smiled to the people who called my name, but did little more than that. For the first half of the game I'd been by myself, wrapped in my goose-down jacket with the fur-rimmed hood that made me look like an Eskimo. It was freezing outside, after it had been unseasonably warm recently, and the pumpkin hot chocolate I'd stopped to buy felt soothing in my hands.

But by the time the second half started, I was standing right in the middle of the group of guys who stood on the sidelines wearing no shirts, something I could scarcely imagine doing with the temperature what it was, each with a letter painted on his chest. I didn't really know any of them, though I knew I'd seen them around. We were cheering together and getting riled up at all the bad calls, our strange camaraderie strengthening with every touchdown.

As the seconds ticked down to the end, our team was a field goal ahead, but the opposing team had the ball. There was every chance that they would win. And if nothing else, I wanted Liam happy. Not only because it would help *our* talk to go better, but also because I genuinely wanted him happy.

The other team was on the five-yard line, six seconds away from the buzzer.

Six. They hiked the ball.

Five. Their quarterback took a few steps back.

Four. He pulled his arm back to throw it into the end zone.

Three. He threw it.

Two. It was in the air, heading straight to where it was meant to go.

One. I saw a body leap into the air, and my heart skipped to see that it was Liam. Interception.

He grabbed the ball and ran victoriously out of the

end zone. The stadium was suddenly a deafening roar. But our section was the loudest. All of the half-naked guys I'd just spent the last two and a half hours with were high fiving, cheering, some giving manly hugs to one another, and then I was being lifted into the air by "G." Then "L," then "A."

I didn't even care that the jacket I was wearing was now covered in green and yellow paint. My throat felt raw from shouting, and I was smiling so hard it hurt my cheeks. But I caught a glimpse of the clock on the scoreboard, and my smile faded. It was eleven-thirty-three. Twenty-seven minutes, and all of this would be gone.

Our players came running back toward the stands, amidst the still-deafening roar of the crowd and the victorious, cheerful sound of the band playing. It sounded just like a last night on earth should sound. Exciting, the air filled with music. Going out with a bang. Even if it wasn't *my* bang, I didn't care. It was a wonderful atmosphere to be in.

I plastered a smile on my face, hoping that the wetness in my eyes looked like overly supportive tears, and clapped as the team ran by.

My eyes were fixed on Liam, who was tailing the group. I held out my hand for a high five as he walked by. Instead, he took my hand and pulled me toward him. The next thing I knew, I was up in the air again. Liam was spinning me around, his arms holding me close to him. Our cheeks pressed together, mine cold and windburned, his warm and soothing. My smile was real now, and I felt happy that at very least, I got to experience this feeling one last time.

He set me down, kissed me on one cold cheek and looked me in the eyes.

"Thanks for being here, Bridget."

He flashed a winning grin and followed his teammates back to the locker room.

My head still whirling, I said goodbye to the half-naked supporters, declined their invitation to go to a "totally awesome party," and told "N" that I'd have to see him do a keg stand another time.

I sat down on the bench I'd been standing on for most of the game. I waited there for twenty minutes, my foot shaking with anticipation and anxiety.

The stadium emptied, the concessions-stand workers pulled down the noisy metal screens for the windows and then I was alone.

Alone to worry. Worry about whether I'd said *I'm sorry* well enough to the people from the boardroom. Worry about the other people I still needed to apologize to. Worry about how my last few moments would feel if I didn't get to say my goodbye to Liam.

Worse than that, I was alone to think and to remember. Maybe this was stupid. Maybe Liam didn't want to hear what I had to say. He had broken up with me, after all, and paid very little attention to me ever since. And I'd spent every single day thinking about how he'd done it.

We'd been watching my favorite old movie, *His Girl Friday,* on the couch in my basement. I remember feeling happy. Feeling terribly content, and satisfied with where I was, and the fact that he was there with me. I remember feeling that even if everything else fell apart, I'd have this. I always had, and I hoped that I would for a long time.

And then he'd paused the movie and scooted forward on the couch. He'd wrung his hands and looked at the floor.

"I don't think I can do this anymore, Bridget," he'd said.

The air had escaped from my lungs. I felt like I'd lost my footing on the edge of the Grand Canyon.

"What?"

"I'm sorry," he'd said quickly. "You've changed, it's just not…you anymore, I guess."

"W-what are you talking about? You've never said anything like this before, what do you mean you can't do it? All of a sudden you have a problem, and it's just… over?" My voice cracked as I said the word.

Over.

Over.

Over.

It was over with Liam.

"It's not out of nowhere for me." He looked at me, but the warmth that was usually in his eyes was gone.

When had it disappeared? How had I missed that?

"Look," he went on, "I've really thought about this, and I just don't want to lose you completely. I think I will if we keep doing this."

I shook my head frantically. "No, Liam, what do you mean it's not out of nowhere? For me, it's *totally* out of nowhere! How long have you been thinking about this? How will breaking up with me keep us from losing each other? This is so *stupid!*" I was growing more hysterical by the second, as he—anyone—could tell.

"Look, of course this isn't what I want either but…I just think it's what has to happen. Maybe sometime in the future things will be different but…right now…"

I gaped at him, unable to speak.

He got up, muttering that he should probably just go.

It's the only time in my life that I can remember begging.

"No, Liam, please!" The words choked out of my chest like bullets. "I'll do whatever, just tell me! You didn't even *talk* to me about this, just…try, please!"

He apologized again, tossed a weary glance my way and walked up the stairs.

I continued to shout at him, my voice wavering desperately as I did so, and he didn't look back. I guess I'm lucky he didn't just turn to me and say, "Frankly, Bridget, I don't give a damn."

As soon as he was out of sight, I burst into tears and cried for hours into the afghan my grandmother had made. The room was lit only by the TV screen, which was paused on a still of Cary Grant for so long I sometimes think I can still see it there, like a ghost.

I cried like that for days. In class, on the way home, in my sleep. I had never thought I'd cry like that over a boy. I'd never thought I was capable of it.

Or, more to the point, thought that a boy would be capable of making me behave that way.

But for the month after he ended it, I went through the five stages of grief in a haze of tears, with a side of seriously over-thinking everything Liam's ending monologue meant or might have implied.

I started with denial and isolation. I shouted over and over to my friends, who were just trying to help, that he would change his mind and call back. Then I told my friends to leave me alone, I had other things to do. What I had to do was to sit in my room, clicking through pictures on my computer and waiting for the phone to ring. Though I think I knew the whole time that it wouldn't. So I don't know if that's really denial, or if it's just hope.

After a few days of him not calling, I got mad at him. Mad that he hadn't called. Mad at how he'd done it. Mad at the choice he'd made by himself, with *no* indication of what was coming. I got mad every time anyone who wasn't Liam called, and mad any time anyone else brought him up or wasn't interested in talking about him.

Then I moved on to what psychologists call "bargaining." Except my begging and bargaining weren't limited to praying or asking God to undo what Liam had done to me. I went so far as to call Liam and promise to be better. Gentleman that he was, he told me calmly that it didn't work that way, and then never mentioned the conversation again.

After having that final assurance that there was no turning back, I'd launched into full-on pajama-sporting, ice cream-eating, puffy-eyed depression. I cried so much in those two weeks that I must have emptied my body of water. In between bouts of crying, I felt nothing else, total indifference to everything, and a numbness that eventually pushed me out of the crying stage.

The fifth step is acceptance. If acceptance means that I continued to live my life and not turn into a shrine-building psychopath, then, sure, I accepted it.

But I didn't necessarily move on. I missed him every day, and my days wove in and out of relapsing into the previous four stages and living a normal life. But still, even as recently as seeing him on the football field, the relationship and the consequential breakup seemed just as present as it ever had.

But maybe it was just *me* who felt that way. Maybe an apology would mean very little to him. Yes, I finally understood it all. He'd been there to watch me change from myself into another person entirely. I finally *got* it. But maybe it was just way too late, and it was all moot. Maybe this wasn't going to be a profound admission, because maybe it just wasn't relevant to him anymore.

Suddenly it seemed obvious that the best thing I could do was just disappear. It was stupid to have come here. I was rapidly feeling more and more embarrassed for having come at all, and like I couldn't get out fast enough. I stood up to leave. And then, of *course,* out he came.

"Hey!" he said, oblivious to my thoughts.

"Hey. Great game, you were really on fire. I couldn't *believe* you got that fumble earlier. And that interception! Man, you were like freaking Larry Fitzgerald out there."

He grinned. "Thanks."

I tried to smile, but instead my eyes and throat began to burn with stupid, poorly timed tears. I tried to hold them back, but I could feel my smile turning into something else.

"Whoa whoa whoa! Bridget, what's goin' on?" His smile died away quickly as he saw my face. He dropped his duffel bag on the ground and put a hand on each of my cheeks. Then, in the way that being with someone comforting always seems to, it became impossible to hold back my tears.

I was crying about everything. The bliss of him and me, the despair of breaking up, the fool I'd made of myself flirting with his friends when we were together, the embarrassment of how I'd been prancing around for the last year and a half, the pain I felt for everyone I'd hurt or insulted and even the fact that I was crying. I was selfish to be here, and especially to be *crying* here. He just won a huge game, and I was here only to bring him down.

I breathed deeply and tried desperately to regain myself. Not to force some illusion of strength, but because I truly was mortified that I'd ever thought this was a good idea.

When I spoke, my voice was an octave higher than usual, and my words were poorly formed. "It's nothing! Please..."

"Come on, Duke, I'm not a moron. Tell me what's going on."

I sniffed and glanced up at the clock. Eleven-fifty-six. He wasn't going to let this go, and it was no time for games. I had to just do it.

"Okay, fine." I took a deep breath. "I've had a revelation. I *have* been a moron. Total moron. And I just wanted you to know that...um...I know that, too."

My words were jumbled. Nothing like the eloquent, articulate speech I'd had planned out in my head.

"Where is this coming from, Bridget?"

"Just...okay, Liam, I know what happened with us.

I changed. I'm not really sure why, but—" another glance at the clock—four minutes left "—I did change, hugely. I became a selfish girl, and all of my values and priorities changed for the worse. It doesn't matter why anymore. I just want you to hear me say I'm sorry. Even if you don't want to accept that, and you have every right to *not* accept it, I just want you to see me here, right now, and hear me when I say that I'm back and that I'm so, so sorry. I ruined all of my friendships and a lot of other things in my life, all with my own hand. But I also ruined us by doing that. And I'm so sorry, Liam. I'm so, so sorry. But I mean, seriously, you probably don't even care, and I also understand that..."

The last half of my messy monologue was said through full-blown, humiliating tears, as Liam watched me curiously, wiping them away with his thumb and listening intently. I looked at his face, taking in his features. Another look at the clock. It was eleven-fifty-seven.

"But now I have to go." I turned on my heel and started running. *I must seem positively out of my mind,* I thought.

"What do you mean you have to go?" He jogged after me.

"I just have to, Liam, please just stay there!" I ran

across the field, my heels catching in the thick grass as I did. Hopping on my right foot, I threw off my left shoe, and then vice versa. I threw them on the ground and ran toward the concessions stand. My face, stinging from my wet tears, turned colder in the freezing wind.

I really hoped that I would just disappear at midnight. It would be weird, but not as weird as it would be if I said I had to go and then I ran behind a shack to die as if on cue.

I heard Liam's footsteps get closer to me. Stupid to think I could outrun the team's MVP. He wrapped a hand around my shoulder and hurried in front of me to stop me from running.

I stopped, breathing hard. I looked behind him at the scoreboard that told me I was two minutes away from whatever was going to happen.

Liam dropped my shoes on the ground and looked very seriously into my eyes.

"Bridget..."

I shook my head frantically and gazed back at him. I felt excruciatingly tense and now, more than ever, tremendously heartbroken.

"There isn't enough time. Please just let me go."

One minute left.

I wanted to turn and run. I didn't know what would happen if I didn't. I didn't know what Liam might witness if I didn't run. What if I exploded, or something equally ridiculous?

But something kept me standing there, unable to move. My feet seemed magnetized to the cold, hard earth.

Within a second, it all changed. One of his hands wrapped gently around the back of my neck and the other went to my waist, pulling me toward him. Then his lips were on mine.

My mind went blank. All I could feel was Liam. For that moment, there was no fear, no regret and no sadness. After all I'd learned about myself, that moment was more than I deserved.

I felt the familiar sensation of the world falling away, and I pulled away from him, terrified that this was it.

I was dying. I was sure of it.

But when I opened my eyes, all I saw was the mystified expression on Liam's face. I looked behind him to see the scoreboard. It was 12:01.

*What?*

"What time do you have?" I asked Liam.

He looked curiously at me, and then down at his watch. "Same as up there. What's wrong with you,

Bridge? You're acting crazy." He didn't sound angry, just worried.

"But I—I'm supposed to be gone!" I stammered. "I figured that at the very least I'd be back in the boardroom."

"Boardroom? What are you talking about?" Liam asked.

"But Anna said that they had to deliberate…and that she'd see me…"

"Who's Anna?"

I turned to him. "Who's Anna?" I repeated. "What do you mean? You know Anna, what are you talking about?"

Liam looked truly confused. "I don't know an Anna. Last Anna I knew was in, like, first grade, and she was only there for a year. Who are you talking about?"

"The new girl, Anna Judge!" My voice was high-pitched and hysterical.

"New girl?"

"Liam, did you hit your head out there?"

He laughed. "No. Are you sure *you* didn't? I know it can get rough in the stands."

"Um. I don't know, maybe I did," I lied, still unable to process the fact that I was still there, and that Liam didn't know who Anna was.

Liam knelt on the ground in front of me.

"Here, give me your foot before it falls off from frostbite."

In a daze, I lifted the foot he was touching. He slipped it into one of my shoes, and tapped my other ankle.

Once I was back in my shoes, he stood and held out an arm.

"Ice cream at my house? You still haven't seen *Animal House* yet, have you?"

I shook my head. "No, not yet."

"All right, let's do it."

We set off toward the parking lot, arm in arm. And then I saw something move out of the corner of my eye.

It was Anna, and she was smiling. My heart sank. I wasn't going to disappear. Anna was either going to take me with her or kill me. I felt stupid for having ever thought that I might get away with living.

She crooked her finger, beckoning me to come to her. Then she backed up into the darkness.

I unlinked my arm and walked to where I'd just seen her.

"Hey—" Liam called, and I heard him take a step toward me.

"No, no, wait one sec." I held up a hand and then walked into the darkness where she'd been.

There she was. She was wearing a black cloak with a wide hood, the kind I'd seen only in old movies.

"So, what now?" I asked, my heart pounding. I was terrified that she was going to tell me to come with her.

"You're okay for right now," she said, and raised an eyebrow.

Relief washed over me. "Thank you…" I didn't know what else to say.

"Be good, Bridget." She smiled, and glanced behind me at Liam.

I turned to where she'd looked, and saw him coming toward me.

"Man, you must have hit your head hard. You ready to go now?"

I looked back for Anna, and she wasn't there.

"But she—"

A movement in the dark again caught my eye.

It was Anna again. She held a finger to her lips to shush me, and then she winked and walked away.

And I knew I'd gotten a stay of execution.

It was over and I had lived.

"Aaand, I'll drive?" He smiled at me, and I couldn't help but smile back.

I didn't know how long I had left, or when or if I'd see Anna again. All I knew was that, until that happened, I wanted to deserve my life.

I still had plenty to make up for.

★★★★★